FIRST COME THUGS, THEN COME MARRIAGE 4

J. DOMINIQUE

First Come Thugs, Then Come Marriage 4

Copyright © 2023 by J. Dominique

All rights reserved.

Published in the United States of America.

Published by Cole Hart Signature, LLC.

Mailing List

To stay up to date on new releases, plus get information on contests, sneak peeks, and more,

Go To The Website Below...

www.colehartsignature.com

CHAPTER ONE
BLESSING

I was numb. I couldn't feel shit, and it sounded as if a siren was going off in my head as I gathered my things from the waiting room so we could go back and see my baby. Golden gave my arm a reassuring squeeze, but it did nothing to make me feel better. My son was in a coma after losing oxygen, and while I should've been relieved that there was some hope of him coming out of it, I couldn't get past him even being in this situation in the first place.

Since they were only allowing two people in to see him at a time, Knight was right by my side. He attempted to take Ky from my arms, and I shook him off, clutching my baby closer. After what happened, I wasn't about to let him out of my sight let alone out of my arms. Thankfully he withdrew, taking a step back so I could move past him. The way I was feeling, it was actually best that he left me alone completely, but I knew that wasn't going to happen. He gave me a wide berth, but I could feel him behind me as I made my way through the double doors after the doctor directed me to Kal's room.

My knees damn near buckled at the sight of him in the makeshift crib hooked up to all types of machines. Silent tears slid down my cheeks as I shuffled closer. The doctor had said they weren't sure why Kal had stopped breathing, but I knew exactly what had happened. There was no doubt in my mind that Angelina had taken out her frustrations on my baby and if Ky hadn't woken up, he would have probably been laying right next to his brother. The thought had me holding him tighter as I looked over Kal's little body in the small hospital gown he was wearing. He looked like he was sleeping peacefully and not in any type of pain, but that didn't make me feel any better. I reached inside the crib and rubbed the back of his little hand, growing pissed off that he wasn't able to grab my finger or reach for me like he normally would.

"This is all your fault," I mumbled lowly, shaking my head as salty tears landed on my lips. His silence let me know he hadn't heard me, so I turned my angry gaze on him and repeated myself, this time much louder. "This is all *your* fault! You let this happen to our baby bringing that fucking demon around us!" His red-rimmed eyes shot from Kal to me, and I watched unbothered as his jaw clenched tightly.

"Lower yo' fuckin' tone before you have these muhfuckas in our business!" he hissed, and I laughed wryly at both the fact that he didn't deny it or that his concern was of someone hearing.

"Nigga, *fuck* you!"

"I'm not bouta do this shit with you here, bruh." He was already shaking his head with a heavy sigh.

Immediately, my eyebrows rose mockingly. "Oh, you wanna wait 'til we get back to the hideout turned crime scene! Naw, you don't wanna do that, what you need to be doin' is finding yo' crazy ass wife!" We hadn't had time to speak on the matter, but we all knew Angelina was behind this, considering what had taken place with her miscarriage and the fact that the bitch was nowhere to be found afterward. I needed that bitch to die, immediately, and while I wanted it to happen as fast as possible, I wanted to be the one to do it. Seeing my baby in the condition he was in had me ready to slit that hoe's throat and watch her body drain of blood. That's how far gone I was, and the only thing I needed Knight to do was bring her ass to me.

We had a silent stare off as he attempted to control his anger while I dared his ass to get stupid with me. It was crazy that we'd literally just made up and already he was right back on my shit list. As pissed off as I was, I also felt a lot of guilt for having been laid up with Knight while that bitch was alone with my baby. I'd been beating myself up since the moment I found Kal and going over every way I could've possibly prevented this. Should I have put up more of a fight when that bitch first popped up at the house? Maybe I should've beat her ass the first time she disrespected me and my kids. I'd gone over every shoulda, woulda, coulda, but nothing was going to rewind the hands of time and bring Kal out of this.

Knight crossed the room in a flash, towering over me, and I defiantly lifted my chin. "We don't need to be discussin' this shit *here*!" he reiterated, making me scoff.

"The whole reason we're here in the first place is because you never wanna discuss shit! We shouldn't even be here! My son shouldn't be laying in this bitch hooked up to all these fucking machines just because of the hoe you decided to marry! Ever since you dragged me back to this muthafucka, it's been one thing after another! I was fine in Atlanta! *We* were fine, and now my father and I are into it, we've got people that want us dead for whatever reason, we're being stalked by yo' ugly ass wife who just tried to kill my fuckin' baby, and you don't even care! You should be out trying to get her ass not in here telling me what the fuck I can and can't sa—"

My sentence was cut off as he threateningly stepped even closer so we were chest to chest with his nostrils flaring. "I know my role in this Bless, I don't need you to remind me of that shit! You think I don't care? You don't think I'm over here wishing I could take his place right now?" He tilted his head, glancing behind me at Kal as his voice cracked before focusing back on me with a look of resolve. "If blood is what you want, I'll give you that. You want Angelina's head, I'll bring that muthafucka to you on a silver platter, but right now all I'm tryna do is sit with my son for a while. Can I just do that without the extra shit?"

Honestly, I was feeling like he didn't deserve the right to be in Kal's presence and I really didn't give a fuck how he felt, but a light tap at the door stopped me from telling him that. A second later, a concerned looking nurse entered the room. She looked between the two of us, taking in the tension before glancing over at Kal, which instantly irritated me. I could already see the judgment clouding her eyes and knew she was thinking the worst of us.

"Is everything alright in here?"

"Yes, we're fine," I said after a few seconds while Knight remained silent. From the slight clenching of his jaw, I knew he was on the verge of snapping on the lady and that was the last thing we needed. Her brows dipped slightly as she shifted her gaze back to Knight.

"Well, we're going to need you guys to keep it down in here. Although he's in a comatose state, Callie doesn't—"

"Ka'Leigh," Knight sneered, interrupting her and causing the lady's eyes to widen.

"I beg your pardon?"

"His name is *Ka'Leigh*. The least you can do is learn your patient's name before trying to come in and tell me what he needs from me." The nurse's face flushed bright red at his tone and she took a timid step backward like she just knew he was about to haul off and beat her ass.

"Sir, there's no reason to get hostile, I was simply suggesting that for Ka'Leigh's wellbeing and the other patients, you keep it down just a bit."

I already knew her using a word like hostile while addressing a Black man was dangerous, especially in our current situation, and before Knight could lay into her any further, I decided to speak up.

"Actually, he was just leaving," I let her know and instantly felt Knight's heated eyes on me. As pissed off as he was though, he didn't try to argue. Instead, he brushed past me with a snort to say a quick goodbye to Kal before disappearing out of the room without another glance in either of our directions. Almost immediately the tension in the room left with him and I breathed a sigh of relief. Hopefully, he used that energy to go find Angelina, because he had me fucked up if he thought I'd be okay with him spending any time with our son while she galivanted around Chicago without a care in the world. My focus was already back on Kal, but I turned back to the nurse with a raised brow when I realized she was still in the room.

"Is there anything else I can do for you?" I frowned, ready to go off if she said anything crazy.

"I was just wondering if you'll be leaving also, because visiting hours will be over soon." She allowed her gaze to fall to Ky as if me having him was reason enough for me to be going home, and I quickly let her know that I wasn't going anywhere.

"I won't be, I'm staying the night, but I would appreciate if you brought an extra blanket or two," I told her with my head cocked to the side, daring her to try and object. Thankfully, she merely pursed her lips together with a nod and went to fetch my blankets, which was in her best interest. Once she finally left the room, I settled into the chair next to Kal and said a silent prayer that God would pull him out of this.

CHAPTER TWO
KNIGHT

I tried my pops's number once again as Bishop drove toward the De'Leon's residence and for the third time the voicemail picked up, eliciting an irritated growl out of me.

"I told you stop tryna call that weird ass nigga! He been movin' funny for a minute and you're the only one who ain't seeing this shit!" Bishop chastised, glaring at me before putting his attention back on the road ahead of us. I didn't want to argue with him about the same damn thing so I instantly shrugged him off, but that didn't mean I wasn't starting to piece shit together on my own. I could admit it was strange to all of a sudden not be able to reach him after weeks of his ass being around nonstop. At the same time, with everything we had going on there was also a good chance some shit had happened to him; it wasn't like it was late enough for his old ass to be asleep.

"I ain't gone lie, Jules said some shit about that nigga being a snake a while back," Rook added from the backseat. "What?" he huffed when Bishop and I shot him a look.

"Nigga, why you just now telling us that shit?" Bishop hissed before I could, making his face ball up.

"Don't be lookin' at me like that! We got a lot of shit going on so it slipped my fuckin' mind!"

"You ain't ask that goofy hoe to elaborate? Fuck type of snake shit could King be on with the De'Leons?" I quizzed, not missing the "duh" look on Bishop's face.

"You don't think it's suspicious as fuck how Angelina's ass popped up at the safe house? Shit, he probably been feeding them information since he came back tryna act like the supportive father! Ain't no telling what else he been doing that's flying under the radar 'cause we're so tied up in other shit." The whole time my brother spoke, I tried to go over any instances where King was acting weird and a few came to mind, yet I still wasn't going to rule out him possibly having gotten caught up with Diego.

"Ayite, I get what y'all sayin', but let's not act like it's not a chance that your girl's husband ain't snatched him up."

"Nigga, really?" Bishop snorted, giving me a look of disbelief while Rook groaned lowly.

"Yeah, really. That's still our pops at the end of the day so I'ma give him the benefit of the doubt just like yo' ass been giving Lovelie. You talkin' all this shit but don't wanna accept that her ass probably had something to do with Deja's shooting!" I shouted just as we pulled up to the De'Leons.

"Awww, here we go." Rook shook his head.

"Just because you and yo' wife's people ain't got no control over her crazy ass don't mean mine dumb enough to cross me," Bishop huffed, pinning me with a look before cutting the car off and lifting his gun from his lap.

"Ain't no way y'all muhfuckas done went from arguing about King to arguing about y'all wives while we tryna put in work," Rook cut in irritably.

"That's his delusional ass."

"I'm delusional 'cause I don't wanna think the worst of our pops?" I quizzed, palming my chest with one hand. Bishop's facial expression gave away that, that's exactly what his ass was thinking. I could admit, I'd always been the one fighting for King's approval, but I didn't think it was crazy to believe in his innocence. It had only been months since we'd lost our mother and now with Kal in a coma, I just couldn't fathom having to kill my father for possibly having a hand in that shit.

"Look, after we leave we can go check on King, but for now, can we get on with this shit? Muhfuckas probably done escaped out a hidden tunnel fuckin' around with y'all niggas!" Rook huffed, opening the back door and placing a foot on the cobblestone driveway. Instead of verbally agreeing, I climbed out, making sure my safety was off before traveling the short distance to their door without waiting for my brothers. The reason for our visit trumped any bullshit we were arguing about and as I rang the bell, I'd already made up in my mind that I was going to kill every single DeLeon if they didn't immediately give up Angelina, damn the consequences. When a few seconds passed without any movement inside the house, I prepared to hit the buzzer again just as Bishop walked up and kicked the door off the hinges with surprising ease. He wasted no time stepping over the threshold with his gun drawn, and I followed closely behind with Rook bringing up the rear.

We moved throughout the lower level clearing each room and coming up empty before ascending the stairs and finding it just as vacant. It was obvious they'd left in a rush and I was almost positive it was because of Angelina, but if he wanted to die along with his daughter that was on him.

"Come on, we gotta go, I know one of these nosy ass neighbors done called the police by now," Bishop finally broke the silence as we met back at the stairs. He looked just as irritated as I felt, but I should've known it wouldn't be as simple as pulling up and snatching their asses. Sending a team over as soon as this shit happened would've been smart, but I was focused on getting my son to the hospital and wasn't really thinking of shit else.

Nodding, I made my way down the stairs behind him and Rook as my phone rang in my pocket. I wasted no time fishing it out just in case it was Blessing with an update on Kal.

"What's up?" I answered without looking. My forehead bunched at the silence I was met with, prompting me to look at the screen just as Angelo's voice came over the line.

"I was expecting a visit from you, but I was hoping it would be on more respectful grou—"

"Fuck respect, DeLeon! You know in this game it's an eye for an eye, so you might as well bring me Angelina and I'll consider calling it even!" I growled as I made it back to the car and ducked inside.

"I think there's something we can work out," he stated calmly like we were talking about something much less evil than his daughter almost killing my son. "How about a sit down tomorrow and we can discuss things moving forward?"

As bad as I wanted to say fuck him and his sit down, I knew meeting with him was the closest I'd get to Angelina. I could feel my brothers eyeing me and probably wondering what was being said, but I kept my focus on the conversation at hand. "Fine, tomorrow at 5," I told him, hanging up so his conniving ass couldn't haggle about the time.

"That nigga said he givin' up Angelina?" Bishop was the first to speak what was on both of their minds, and I slowly shook my head. "Fuck you meeting with him for then? Ain't shit gone get accomplished in a sit down but me blowing his fucking face off!"

"We need him to lead us to her, after that, I don't give a

fuck what you do to him," I said truthfully. Little did Bishop know, but I'd already made up my mind they were all going to die behind Angelina's actions. Who killed who wasn't my concern as long as I got my target. I'd promised Blessing that bitch's head and I fully intended to deliver.

For the first time that day I saw the semblance of an evil smile creeping up on my brother's face. Murder stayed on that nigga's mind and between Deja leaving his ass and his nephew being harmed, I knew he was ready to go on a spree.

Seemingly satisfied with the promise of Angelo's life, he drove the rest of the way to our pops's crib without any more issues. When we pulled up and saw his cars all parked out front along with a fully lit up house, we shared a look before climbing out. I let us all in with my key, unsure of what we'd find on the other side of the door. We spread out with me heading straight for his office while Bishop checked the rest of the floor and Rook traveled upstairs. Unlike the rest of the house, his office was blanketed in darkness and as soon as I flipped the light switch, I realized why. Right in the middle of the floor lay Aunt Milly. The puddle of blood that pooled around her head let me know there was no helping her, and I immediately cursed. I looked around, hoping I'd see something to give me an idea of what had taken place, but aside from her lying dead in the middle of the floor there wasn't shit else abnormal about the room.

"Yo, what the fuck! Is that Milly?" Rook's loud ass entered as I dropped onto the leather couch in the corner and swept a hand down my face.

"Yeah." I sighed defeatedly, unsure of what else to say. King was looking more and more like a snake and although it didn't make any sense why he would kill his sister-in-law, her lying dead in his office was suspicious as fuck. Rook was just as at a loss for words as I was and he let out a low groan, dropping into the seat beside me.

"I know this muhfucka didn't!" I kept my head down, not wanting to look into Bishop's accusing eyes. A second later, a loud thud followed by glass shattering let me know his crazy ass had punched a hole in the wall, knocking down some of the pictures there. "I told yo' ass! We should've been handled this nigga and now he done killed the last living connection to our fuckin' mama! I swear to God I'ma kill that nigga, I don't give a fuck what you say!" he continued going off while Rook and I remained silent. As bad as I wanted to try and argue our pops's innocence, it was just too much shit stacked against him. All I could do was hope there was an explanation for this shit and that King was being held hostage somewhere. That thought immediately went out the window when Rook's phone went off and he stood up in a rush.

"We gotta go, Golden's ass slipped security!"

CHAPTER THREE
BLESSING

I 'd been at Kal's bedside since the night before, watching closely for any signs of life and growing disappointed every time there was none. Despite him being nonresponsive, the nurses were still coming in and out of the room frequently, either checking his vitals, emptying his catheter, or fiddling with the numerous machines in the room, and I made sure to keep a close eye on them as well. It was beyond me that someone would be sick enough to harm a defenseless baby, but now that a bitch had, I didn't trust a soul around my son. Either of them. All of the nurses had offered to keep an eye on Ky while I went to the bathroom or to get something to eat, and I refused them every time. It was obvious that they weren't safe out of my sight and I intended to make sure they never were.

Light tapping at the door had me sitting up straighter, prepared for one of the nurses or doctors to enter the room, but when I turned around Knight was walking through the door with my overnight bag in hand. Unlike me, he looked well rested and freshly showered, instantly pissing me off, and

I rolled my eyes at the sight of him. Ky, on the other hand, immediately began chanting his name and trying to climb over me to reach him. The petty side of me wanted to hold onto him tighter and not allow him to go to his father, but I handed him over. As soon as he was in Knight's arms, he settled down, entertaining himself by playing with his daddy's thick beard. It was a heartwarming moment, except I couldn't enjoy it knowing that one of the members of our family was absent.

"Bless, I—" he started, but I quickly interrupted whatever the fuck he was about to say.

"Did you find her?" I asked, raising a brow, and his face fell, silently giving me his answer. "I don't want to hear shit until you do what you promised." A pregnant pause fell over the room as a slew of different emotions flashed across his face.

"I'm not tryna argue with you today, Blessing. I just came to visit the boys and bring yo' ungrateful ass a change of clothes," he said dryly, tossing the bag down by my feet and making his way to the other side of Kal's bed. I looked between him and the bag with my nose turned up. The last thing I was thinking about at the moment was changing my damn clothes. Truthfully, from the moment we arrived at the hospital, I'd made it up in my mind that I wasn't going to do shit until my baby came up out of his coma. Instead of telling him that though, I kicked the bag aside and folded my arms over my chest.

"If it ain't Angelina's head in that muhfucka, then I don't want it."

He'd already put his attention back on Kal, but when I said that his dark eyes shot over to me and his face twisted into a deep scowl. "Yo, I get that you mad, shit, I'm mad too, but stop talkin' like that around them. I already told you, you can't be saying shit like that in here," he stressed, letting his eyes roll around the room like he was worried that there was a recording device in there, and I waved him off.

"Are you really though? 'Cause instead of finding that bitch, you're in here giving me a lesson on how to be a criminal!" I felt myself about to lose control of my emotions and quickly took a couple of deep breaths. I was turning into someone that I didn't even recognize, but I couldn't stop myself. There was a rage brewing inside me and I was ready to unleash it on any and everyone that came in contact with me, Knight being the main target.

I could tell he was stunned by me accusing him of not being mad about Kal just by the stupid look on his face. He stared at me blankly, probably searching for the right words to address me, just as someone knocked on the door snatching our attention. I wasn't surprised to see the same nurse that had introduced herself to me that morning, but what did give me pause was the doctor coming in behind her along with an older woman in a wrinkled pantsuit and a police officer. My eyebrow instantly hiked as they all shuffled into the room silently before the doctor finally stepped up to speak.

"Good afternoon, Mr. and Mrs. Grand." He nervously looked between us, and instead of correcting him, I eyed the two oddballs in the room. The police were already a red flag, but the lady was even more so and I immediately got a bad feeling. "This is my associate, Latoya Fields, from Child Protective Services—"

"Wait, why is DCFS here when I was told this was an unexplained occurrence?" I shrilled, frantically shifting in my seat. "And why are the police here with her! I know you muthafuckas don't think I did this to my baby!" Now I could no longer sit still, and I hopped to my feet, noticing the shift in their demeanors from the sudden movement.

"Blessing, *chill*," Knight voiced sternly, but I wasn't trying to hear that. My heart pounded in my chest as tears blurred my vision.

"No! They're trying to say we hurt Kal! Bitch, did you call them and say I did this shit!" I turned my attention to the nurse, whose eyes widened and she took a step backward. "Was it that nurse from last night? Where is she!"

"Mrs. Grand, I need you to calm down. No one is accusing you of anything." The doctor moved so that he was standing in front of the nurse with his arms outstretched as if protecting her from me, while the police officer shuffled forward with his hand on his belt. Within seconds, Knight was by my side staring him down.

"All that ain't necessary," he addressed the officer, and despite his badge and gun, the man was visibly shook from Knight's large frame being so close.

"None of this is necessary, Mr. Grand. I'm simply here to conduct an investigation per protocol. Your wife's erratic behavior over the last twenty-four hours and now in my presence has raised concern among the hospital staff, and it is their responsibility to report such things." As she spoke, I shot daggers at both the doctor and nurse. I could admit that I hadn't been myself, but I'd almost lost my son and I'd have hoped they'd understand that, but clearly they hadn't. Instead of seeing the situation for what it was, they immediately assumed the worst and had called social services on me.

"Erratic? Our son is in a coma! You wouldn't be frantic having to go through that?" Knight spoke up, and I snorted inwardly. This was all his fault and I wished I could have just thrown Angelina's ass under the bus, but then I wouldn't be able to see her take her last breath, and that was much more important than proving to these people that I wasn't the one responsible for Kal's injuries.

"Listen, I understand, but I still need to do my job and in

the meantime, you both need to allow me to complete my investigation without interference. Effective immediately, we need you both to leave the premises and not return until I contact you." I swear it felt like all the breath left my body. As if sensing that I was about to lose it, Knight gripped my hand tightly.

"So, we're not allowed to even visit him? How long will this take? What if he takes a turn for the worse while you have us banned?" I shot off question after question, spiraling even more as realization set in. These people were trying to separate me from my baby when he needed me most. I was sure he'd rather see his mother when he came to than a bunch of strangers that didn't give a fuck about him. Latoya blinked, unmoved, like she'd been dealing with these types of situations for years and couldn't care less about any of my questions.

"At this time, I don't believe it's in Ka'Leigh's best interest to be alone with either of you. I will see if supervised visitation will be permitted after I conduct interviews with you and the staff. Until then, you need to turn over your visitation bands," she said in a monotone voice and motioned for the nurse who'd miraculously produced a pair of scissors. Aghast, I looked into each of their emotionless faces while Knight asked for her supervisor's name and number and informed them that we'd be in contact with our lawyer. Him having a level head rubbed me the wrong way. How could he be so calm when they were basically taking away our ability to be there for Kal?

"Are you seriously about to let them kick us out?" I quizzed, getting more distraught as he held out his wrist and allowed the nurse to cut off his visitor band.

"We don't have a choice right now Bless, just let them get the band and give me some time to make a few calls, ayite." He tried to grab ahold of my hand to relax me, and I instantly snatched away.

"No! They're gonna have to drag me out this muthafucka because I refuse to just abandon my baby!" My outburst caused Ky to begin crying, and I was suddenly reminded of his presence in the room. Going into protective mode, I reached for him and got my feelings hurt when he clung to Knight instead.

Realizing that he was the calmest, Latoya addressed Knight, handing him a business card. "Mr. Grand, I'll be in touch. In the meantime, I ask that you not make any attempts to return." With a nod, she stepped aside, giving the officer room to come closer, and he approached me, ready to use physical force.

"I got her." For the first time since they'd arrived, Knight seemed to have my back, placing a protective arm out in front of me to block him. "Come on Bless, let them do their jobs and I promise we'll be back before the end of the week." I wanted to curse them all out. I wanted to tear up the hospital room and beat Latoya and the nurse's asses. Hell, I wanted to beat Knight's big ass for making another promise he likely wouldn't keep, but at the risk of losing Ky also, I merely nodded and allowed him to guide me past the group as silent tears rolled down my face.

CHAPTER FOUR

KNIGHT

I was beyond stressed. Not only was my son in the hospital by way of my wife and I wasn't even allowed to see him, but Milly was dead and it was possible my father had done it. Considering that we still had yet to hear from him or Diego, it was becoming more and more likely that he had, which was even more fucked up because we wouldn't be able to bury her like normal. We'd had the cleanup crew sweep the house and make it so it didn't look like shit had gone down there. Since we couldn't go the usual route as far as a funeral, I'd hit up my niggas Dinero and Cash to handle things discreetly at their funeral home. We'd settled on a small memorial service before she'd get cremated, which Bishop wasn't too happy about, but we really didn't have much of a choice. I had enough problems considering the decline Blessing had been on since we'd gotten removed from the hospital. She'd gone from spazzing on me every time I said anything to her to barely speaking to me or anybody else. It'd gotten so bad that I called Ava and she came over on the first flight out with no questions asked. She'd arrived a couple hours before, and after cursing me out, she'd been under her cousin ever since. Her presence gave me a little bit of relief knowing someone would be there with her and Ky while I went to meet up with Angelo.

I stepped into our bedroom where Ava was trying to force feed Blessing a sandwich while Ky played at her feet with one of his toys. At the sight of me, they both rolled their eyes but I was only stopping through to check on them and give Ky some love before I left. There was no telling how this meeting would go and I didn't want to speak into existence my death, but there was a chance shit could get crazy. He'd been focusing on making the lights flash when he noticed me and began chanting my name, immediately garnering a smile despite my mood. It never got old hearing either of them say 'Dada,' and I was hoping that soon I'd be hearing them both say it.

I swooped him up and planted a kiss on top of his curly head before hugging him to me tightly. Ava had just recently given him a bath so he was smelling sweet like lavender and whatever other baby fresh shit she'd used. That along with the soft ass pajamas he had on was a whole vibe, and I wished I could stay and spend time with him instead of a group of men I hated.

"Are you gonna be long?" Ava asked, interrupting the tender moment.

"Hopefully not. What's up, you need something?" Sighing, she sat the half-eaten sandwich aside and sat up on the side of the bed. I took in Blessing, who had since closed her eyes in an effort to avoid me. In just two days she had changed so much that she barely looked like herself. Her usually supple skin looked ashen, and her hair was all over her head. Even though she'd allowed me to escort her from the hospital and into our new home, that was where her compliance ended. She'd crawled straight into bed and refused to let me help her into the shower or a change of clothes. I could already see this going downhill fast if I wasn't able to get our lawyer on this DCFS shit. I'd already put in a couple of calls and was waiting on a reply, and I hoped between him and the supervisor down at the social services office that I'd be hearing something soon.

"Actually, I have a list. There ain't shit in this house. She needs some toiletries and maybe something to help her sleep. I put in an order for groceries but that's already going to be over an hour wait, so if you don't think you can beat that let me know." She hesitantly held out a piece of loose-leaf paper that was full front to back with the items she was requesting.

"I got you," I promised without knowing whether I'd be able to come through. The truth was I didn't really have time to be out here shopping and shit, but I was trying to handle business and be there for Blessing.

"Don't play Knight, if you don't think you can do it, let me know now." The warning look she gave didn't stop me from taking the paper as I assured her that I'd take care of it.

"I got it handled, Ava." I didn't mean for it to come out as harsh as it did, but I couldn't help being a little annoyed. As a grown ass man, the last thing I needed was for another person to doubt my word. It was bad enough Blessing was demanding Angelina's head and now for me to work miracles with DCFS, some hygiene products were the least of my troubles at the moment. Ignoring the glare she sent my way, I kissed my son again and gave him another quick hug before setting him back on the floor.

"I'll be back soon," I told her, leaning over our large bed so I could kiss Blessing's mean ass too. She may not have been fucking with me, but I wasn't going to let that stop me from showing her affection. As soon as my lips landed on her forehead, her eyes snapped open and she gave me an icy look. "I know you're not fuckin' with me right now, but I love you and I'll see you in a little bit." I was sure she didn't understand the meaning behind my words, but I said them anyway, hoping that she never would. As mad as she was, she still didn't speak to even say fuck me, and I backed away with a sigh. Ava gave me an encouraging look but it did nothing to make me feel any better as I grumbled a goodbye and left.

I was still in a fucked-up mood by the time I met up with my brothers a short while later and I wasn't trying to hide it. I pulled up beside their cars and stepped out coolly, making sure the safety was off my gun before tucking it behind my back.

"You cool, bro?" Rook quizzed, looking at me curiously when I reached them.

"I'm straight man, let's just get this shit over with," was my answer, even though I was far from okay. I was sure my tardiness and lack of a suit were the reasons for his question, but I wasn't in the right headspace for any of the formalities I usually put on. They shared a look, keeping whatever they were thinking to themselves, and I brushed past them. As usual, when there was a meeting the small bar was deserted with only our cars and those of Angelo's present.

"Good evening, fellas," Meechie greeted us with a nod and waved us in. Without even looking, I knew my brothers were confused but neither of them questioned why he was allowing us in with our weapons. I hadn't mentioned I'd had a conversation with Meechie earlier that day and we came to an understanding. Having lost his wife to the game, he was well aware of the need for revenge on the person who harmed your family. Angelo had done a good job of keeping what his daughter had done under the rug, but I was going to bring that shit to light. He knew better than anybody that it was rules to this shit, and harming a child was something that was highly frowned upon.

I rounded the corner and smirked at the sight of Angelo

flanked by his men. He'd opted to bring a couple more than last time, as if that would help him.

"Knight," he addressed me as I took the seat across from him.

"Skip the pleasantries Angelo, where that bitch at?" Bishop spoke before I could, making Angelo's jaw go slack.

The cool demeanor he'd been putting on instantly dropped and his face reddened. "No need for name calling, that *bitch* you speak of is my daughter!"

"So, nigga, fuck you and that bitch! You know she fucked up for what she did!" Rook snapped, lunging for him, and I quickly held him back as Angelo's men moved closer, but the sight of my gun halted them. I wasn't in the mood to fight considering that we were outnumbered, and I damn sure wasn't trying to argue. Even Angelo looked shook at me having a gun, and he instantly searched for Meechie to no avail.

"What is this? Weapons have no place here!" Although his voice was high-pitched, he sat back in his seat tensely.

"*This* is a muhfucka who knows right from wrong trying to right a situation," I spoke of Meechie with a shrug. "Knowing how your daughter violated, you should be the first one making sure she atones for her mistakes. My son is in the hospital fighting for his life right now and it's Angelina's fault. Now I've tried to ask nicely, shit, I even tried to give you a chance to do the right thing, but since you want to keep playing I'm demanding you tell me where the fuck is Angelina!" My nostrils flared as I pointed the gun in his face. Angelo stared down the barrel as my brothers followed suit, upping their guns to hold his men off. After a few seconds, he suddenly smirked and relaxed in his chair.

"If we're all to atone to our roles, then the very first person you need to be looking for isn't Angelina, it's your father, pendejo." His grin widened and he tilted his head sinisterly after seeing the initial shock on my face as he confirmed what we already suspected. "You didn't know? King's been trying to help us get Angelina back in her rightful place as your wife ever since that *perra negra* came back with those bastards! If you want somebody to blame, blame hi—" Whatever else he was about to say was silenced as I sent multiple bullets into his head. Without hesitation, my brothers unloaded on his men as well, and suddenly the room fell silent.

"I see everything went as planned." Meechie appeared, looking from us to the damage with a raised brow. I'd already slipped him some cash for whatever ended up destroyed in the process of our meeting, so he was probably already calculating that shit in his head as he looked around.

"Yeah, besides his bitch ass not tellin' me shit," I grumbled. Although we'd gotten clarity on King, who was now added to my hit list, I still didn't have a location on Angelina.

"Don't worry, with daddy gone she's bound to come out of hiding if for nothing else but to get some type of protection." Meechie patted my back as a group of men in blue hazmat suits came in and went to work cleaning up the scene. "Let me know if you need anything else though. You know I got a soft spot for kids, so I'm gone make sure I keep my ear to the streets for you too." I shook his hand with a nod and he escorted us back out so his crew could finish.

"Nigga, you could've told us what the fuck was up before we got in there," Bishop huffed as we all walked back to our cars.

"My bad, it was some last-minute shit, but now that we know King's ass was in on this shit, what we gone do?"

Of course, Bishop was the first to speak. "You already know I been wanted that nigga's head." He shrugged, and I looked over at Rook who did the same.

"Ain't no room for disloyalty so his ass gotta go." I'd been the main one caping for King while they'd both been suspicious of him from the jump, so I already figured they'd quickly come up with the decision to take him out. While I was still in disbelief that the man who'd raised us could've had anything to do with harming his own grandchild, I was prepared to do what was necessary. Kal deserved that plus more.

"Ayite, we gone ice him out and see if he does some stupid shit to get caught up. He ain't got that much of a head start so he probably spending all cash. Bishop, hit up your tech guy and see if he can track his cards just in case. In the meantime, I gotta make a run for Ava since it ain't shit at the crib right now, but I'll get up with y'all bright and early," I let them know and headed toward my car. I was surprised they both let me make it without saying some smart shit but at the same time, I was sure it had more to do with them being in shock that King was actually that much of a snake. No doubt even our OG was turning over in her grave, and Milly would've been too if it wasn't for the fact that she couldn't be buried. King had fucked me up with this shit, but just like he'd gone against his family without any remorse, I was going to do the same thing to him but much worse. Shaking off the events, I made my way to the closest store to do what I'd promised, feeling somewhat closer to granting Blessing's wishes.

CHAPTER FIVE
ANGELINA

"This is bullshit! I should've known this wasn't a surprise vacation when y'all made me get out of bed to leave! Now we're stuck here and can't get in touch with Daddy all because you can't control yourself!"

I half listened to Jules fuss as I laid in bed trying to come up with a plan. Yes, we were stuck out in the middle of nowhere and hadn't heard from our papa in days, so it was safe to assume that he was either being held captive or dead. The way the Grand men worked had me believing the latter but I didn't regret what I'd done, only that I wasn't able to complete the job. Why should Blessing have been able to still have her boys when I couldn't even hold or see my baby? After all of the hell Knight had put me through, they both deserved to suffer and I wasn't going to stop until I felt like their pain was equal to mine. It was obvious I'd have to brainstorm with Mama though, because Jules wasn't doing shit but complaining and I was in too much pain to argue with her.

"Ughh! How can you just lay there when Daddy could be

hurt!" Jules's voice cut through my thoughts and I let out a low groan.

"SHUT UP! All you've been doing since we got here is complain! Does your mouth ever get tired of moving? Why don't you do something useful and try to find me something for pain. I am trying to heal after losing my baby!" I ignored the sharp pain that shot through my side and down to my pussy from shouting. My best bet was to use the sympathy card with her because she didn't seem to respond to anything else. Just as I expected, her face filled with concern and she finally closed her mouth.

"I watched some videos about the procedure," she said lowly, sliding onto the foot of the bed. "Was it as bad as they all said?"

It had only been a couple of days since finding out my baby girl was dead and having to get her body sucked out of me. Against my primary's wishes, the very first thing I did when we touched down in the Hamptons was visit a clinic. There was no way I was going to walk around for an extended period of time with a dead fetus in me. They were sick to even suggest such a thing and honestly, I felt like I should sue for emotional damage. If I wasn't on the run from my estranged husband, it was definitely something I would've looked into because we'd be needing all the money we could get.

Sighing at the thought of how much more difficult things were about to become, I adjusted the pillow I had tucked between my legs and let my eyes flutter closed. "No, I don't even remember the surgery part, just waking up cramping and bleeding. This empty feeling inside knowing that my baby isn't there anymore is the worst part," I admitted as a lone tear slipped out of my eye. Even the loss of Knight hadn't been so heart wrenching, and I felt like he and his little bitch were fully responsible from having me stressed over the last few months.

I was hoping that at this point they were both so overcome with grief that they couldn't function, at least then they'd feel a semblance of what I was going through.

"Oh no, I didn't mean to make you cry! I'll go get your medicine and some ice cream." She was already climbing to her feet as she spoke and I nodded, giving her a raspy 'okay' in response. As soon as she was out of the room I breathed a sigh of relief. Jules was exhausting, and having been out from under the same roof as her had clearly made me forget that fact. While she always made it a point to blame me over Rook's rejection, I was beginning to think it was her personality because I couldn't stand to be around her for more than a few minutes at a time. With her out of the room I thought over our options. My father had a few men there with us, but they were nowhere near enough to go up against Knight and his brothers. I needed to know what they had up their sleeves if anything, and my only way to get that information was to call King again. I hadn't talked to him since I left the safehouse and that was only because I needed help escaping. God had to be on my side because he was already on his way when I called and I was able to quickly get out of dodge. He'd been there every step of the way in our planning of killing Blessing and the twins, but Rook's drama with Diego had somewhat thrown a monkey wrench in things.

At this point though, I was willing to team up with Diego's ass just to give us numbers, which was another reason I needed to get in touch with King. With that thought in mind, I reached for my phone and scrolled until I came across his contact. I impatiently waited for him to answer and when he did, I didn't miss the annoyance in his tone.

"What now!" he hissed with his mouth close to the speaker, and my head instantly jerked back. He should've been the last one with an attitude, but I chalked it up to whatever was going on with his sons and I immediately got excited, hoping it was Kal's death.

"You were supposed to keep me posted on what was going on out there. My father went to meet with your sons and I haven't heard from him since. Do you know anything about that?" I hinted with raised brows. His almost whispering tone and quiet background gave me reason to believe that he was around Knight, and I giddily pressed my ear against the phone just in case I could hear him in the background. It was crazy how far my obsession had gone but I was in too deep at this point.

"I don't know shit about shit! I'm laying the fuck low and I hope you are doing the same! I can guarantee that if your father hasn't returned then he won't be after what you did, so you better be getting as far away as you can before your ass comes up missing next!" Before I could respond he hung up, leaving my jaw on the floor. I was baffled as to why he was laying low and how he didn't know what had transpired with my father. He hadn't given me much of anything and I immediately called him right back only to be met with his voicemail.

"I know his ass didn't just block me," I grumbled, gearing up to try again when my sister popped back in the room juggling a glass of water, my meds, and a bowl of ice cream as promised. I rushed to end the call as she began setting everything up on the side table, rambling about me having something on my stomach to go with the medication. Any appetite I may have had was gone after talking to King but just as I was about to tell her that, our mother came flying into the room in a rage. She damn near threw Jules out of the way as she stormed over to me and literally slapped a blood clot out my ass. Stunned for the second time in minutes, I held my stinging jaw while Jules tried to hold her back. She was rapidly screaming at me in Spanish and Jules and I both caught on to what she was saying at the same time. Gasping dramatically, Jules released her as her eyes began filling with tears.

"This is *your* doing! You did this!" She shoved her phone in my face, showing me a picture of my father's unrecognizable body. Vomit erupted from my throat and covered my blanket at his mutilated corpse. Despite everything I'd said, I was still hopeful that the powerful Angelo DeLeon was for sure coming back, but now with evidence of his demise I was riddled with emotion. Aside from my mother, my father was the only person who always had my back and now he was dead from trying to protect me. If I hadn't been hellbent on revenge before I definitely was now, and I didn't care what I had to do. I was going to make the Grand family pay for this.

CHAPTER SIX
DEJA

I'd been holed up in a hotel for a few days just in case Bishop was lying about letting me go, but so far I hadn't seen or heard from him or anybody else for that matter. While I was low key hurt that no one had reached out, I was going to take it as a sign that God was removing negativity from my life. Now the only thing left to do to fully cut ties with that nigga was to terminate my pregnancy, but that shit was much easier said than done. I could talk shit all day but the truth was, I didn't want to be the type of woman that would get an abortion just to spite a nigga. Then again, giving myself an out from a possible eighteen-plus years of hell was a form of protecting my mental health. I'd gone back and forth so much over the last few days that I didn't even want to think about it anymore. Hopefully, I had enough time to actually weigh my options.

I moved about my hotel room, grabbing all of my things with Baby right on my heels completely unaware of what was going on. He was another piece of Bishop's married ass that I should've ridded myself of, but if my hesitation with him was any indication then I already knew when it came down to it I would keep the baby too. Disgusted with myself for being so weak, my jaw tightened as I threw my toothbrush into my bag. I definitely needed to get my mind right and the best way to do that would be to visit my granny, but first I needed to go home and stop by my studio. It seemed like it'd been forever since I was behind a camera lens and I knew if nothing else got me right, then doing what I loved certainly would.

A few minutes later I was heading out the door with Baby under one arm and my bag under the other. After checking out, I loaded us up in the car and headed toward home. Even with my music playing loudly I still couldn't stop my mind from wandering back to Bishop and wondering why he'd allowed me to leave when we were all supposedly in danger. It had me thinking his crazy ass really didn't care, and that hurt more than knowing he'd married his weak ass wife. Even if he didn't care though, I'd been protecting myself for a long time and all I needed to do was get another gun, which I planned to do once I was settled in.

I pulled up on my block twenty minutes later and my brows dipped seeing an open house sign in my yard along with multiple people standing around. There wasn't anywhere to park near my actual house so I double parked and hopped out, ready to curse everybody's ass the fuck out. Sore body and all, I stormed up the walkway, kicking the sign as hard as I could as I passed. It flew to the ground, gaining the attention of the people that were close by.

"This house is not for sale so if you don't live here, get the fuck out my yard!" I shouted, growing even more pissed off when they didn't all immediately scatter. "*Now!* I ain't playin'!" I waved my hands wildly before stomping up the porch while they all looked at me like I was some crazy person. I literally had to be living in the twilight zone because there was no way my house that I hadn't even been in was full of potential buyers. Just as I reached the door, Larry appeared with a young white couple, but his smile quickly disappeared and his eyes widened upon seeing me, making my rage boil over. I should've known my sister and her weasel of a husband were behind this shit. She'd been trying to get me to sell constantly but I never thought she'd go behind my back during my weakest moment to actually go through with the shit. I was beyond hurt, but I was mainly pissed off.

"Oh Deja, um, I wasn't expecting you," Larry stuttered, looking at the time on his raggedy watch. Suddenly he was sweating bullets and adjusting his tie.

"Mmhm, I bet yo' bitch ass didn't! What the fuck do you have goin' on here? 'Cause it looks like you're trying to sell a property that doesn't belong to you, and if you or any of these people don't want to catch a bullet in the next five seconds, I suggest you get them the fuck out of here!" At the sound of bullets flying, the couple along with everyone else quickly fled, no longer interested in trying to gentrify my block while he stood there stuttering.

"I, uh your m-mom and sister said—"

"I don't give a fuck what they said! Neither of their names are on the deed and you better hope I don't put y'all grimy asses behind bars for this shit!" I fumed, wanting so badly to slap the glasses off his face, but I settled at pushing him aside so I could make sure everyone was out ignoring the quiet 'thank God' he mumbled as I passed. He really had a whole set up with a white-clothed table full of cookies, drinks, and finger foods all set off to the side while a list of *my* home's amenities sat on easel near the kitchen. The classical music that was playing as I ventured further inside explained why he didn't immediately hear me yelling outside. "Oh, these muthafuckas got me fucked up!" I said under my breath as I walked through, checking to make sure my equipment that was still laid out hadn't been touched. Before I could get to my bedroom though, I heard the unmistakable voice of my sister going off and within seconds, she'd stormed her way inside with her goofy ass husband and my mama in tow. She really had the nerve to look upset like she wasn't in the wrong. My eyes zeroed in on her ensemble, noting that she was rocking designer from head to toe. If the gawdy Fendi print wasn't obvious enough, the material instantly gave away that it wasn't her usually fake threads, and I couldn't help but wonder if she'd maxed out a credit card just to flex one outfit.

"What do you think you're doing? It took all day to put together this set up and now you've probably scared off all our potential buyers!"

"Hun, I—" Larry tried to grab her attention but I cut his timid ass off.

"*Our*? Bitch, is you crazy? This is my house and I've told you multiple times that I don't want to sell!" Shock filled her face and she instantly clamped her mouth shut. While she tried to gather herself, my mama stepped around her and decided to speak up.

"You got your memory back?" she noted, looking me over curiously. For some reason, her reaction irritated me more, and I nodded with a hard eye roll.

"Yes Ma, a couple days ago, and I think it's fucked up that you would let them do some shit like this while I was recovering! What was y'all even gone tell me if you were able to sell it? You were just gone let me come back to nothing and have to sleep in my studio?" I hadn't been expecting an answer but the way the two shared a look had my chest ready to cave in.

"Actually, *you* told me to sell them both when you got out of the hospital. Don't you remember?" my mama finally dragged out, like she was trying to ease the news on me, and

my heart shattered. I knew that we didn't have the best rela-
tionship, but I never would've expected her to lie about some
shit like that and I had to wonder why.

Chuckling in disbelief, I shook my head at her. "You know
damn well...Why Mama? Why would you try to sell the two
things I cherish more than anything in this world? You know I
would never do that." I didn't realize I was crying until I tasted
my salty tears. We'd always been at odds but I still couldn't
believe she'd try to stab me in the back like that.

"Oh please Deja, stop with the theatrics!" she huffed,
waving a dismissive hand. "It's not that serious. If you don't
want to sell then fine! We were really just trying to do you a
favor, but fuck it! I swear you're just like your granny with that
flip flopping shit! I'll send your cut of the money from the
studio sale and we can just call it even—"

I could no longer hear after she said studio and sale in the
same sentence, and I instantly lunged for her without even
thinking about it. Caught off guard, she was unable to defend
herself as I sent blow after blow to her face and head. Between
her screams I could hear Drea talking shit as Larry tried to hold
her back. I was low key hoping he would because I planned to
do the same thing to her that I was doing to our mama. As if
she read my mind, she somehow managed to wiggle free of her
husband's hold and as soon as I saw her looming in my periph-
eral vision, I slung my mama aside. I'd been waiting for the
opportunity to beat Drea's ass for a while and I didn't hesitate
to snatch her up by the collar of her shirt and began pounding
her face in.

"Get off her!" Larry shrieked as we moved around going
blow for blow. When I felt myself being pulled away roughly, I
began kicking, sending her flying backward, and she landed on
top of our mama who was still trying to climb to her feet.
Seeing his wife on the floor had Larry literally dropping me on

my ass, and I winced from the impact but still managed to pick myself up just in case any of them wanted more. It suddenly made sense why they were decked out in designer and were now trying to sell my damn house. Likely there wasn't any more money left over from the sale and my mama was just stalling for time. I angrily paced the floor, still filled with adrenaline as Larry helped them both to their feet.

"Hurry up and get those bitches the fuck out my house before I call the police and say y'all muthafuckas attacked me knowing I'm pregnant!"

"Girl, fuck you! Technically you don't have a house because you signed the deed over to Mama, so we don't gotta go nowhere!" Drea looked at me smugly and dusted off her clothes. I wasn't even surprised by her admission at this point. Obviously, they'd had to forge my signature for the sale of the studio, so it was safe to assume she'd done the same with the house. I'm not sure what she was expecting, but the deep, gut-wrenching laugh that came out had her brows knitting. Nodding as my laughter died down to a chuckle, I held up a finger.

"Okay, hold that thought." I left them standing there looking confused as I stormed off to my bedroom, talking shit in my head the whole way. The fact that nobody came after me or immediately ran was comical, but I definitely had some-thing for all their asses. Reaching my closet, I clicked on the light and began tossing aside shoe boxes and purses until I found what I was looking for. I smiled as I pulled my granny's old ass revolver out of the box I kept her favorite things in. For sure, she'd always kept it on her, which was a big reason why I'd done the same with my own and I was so glad I hadn't packed it away in the basement. Checking to make sure it was loaded, I let out a satisfied grunt and headed back to where my "family" was still standing around. The outstretched gun was the first thing they noticed upon my return though and they all scrambled to get out of the door, damn near knocking each other down in the process. Just for shits and giggles, I let off a round and cackled at the screams they emitted as I followed behind them. The way I felt, I wanted to put a bullet in each of their asses, but I let them make it to their car and watched as they pulled away on two wheels. I couldn't even feel accomplished though because I was still out of a studio and they still held the deed to my house, but if they thought it was over, they were very mistaken. If I didn't do shit else, I was going to get my shit back or end up in jail trying.

CHAPTER SEVEN
BISHOP

The last thing I should've been doing was looking into what happened to Deja after the way she left, but when Lucky called and said he had street footage of the accident, I immediately told him to send it over. While I fully intended to find and kill whoever had been stupid enough to go after her, a part of me also wanted to prove to my brothers that Lovelie wasn't a part of the shit. I wasn't ready to accept that she'd gone over her father's head and had been able to get one over on me. Considering who I was, that shit was just unacceptable. Plus, I hated to admit I was wrong.

The video came through just as I was pulling up at Knight's crib, and I paused, stepping out so I could view it alone. He'd cut it so that only the part right before the accident started playing and I watched silently as a black Denali sped up on Deja's security, sending them veering off the road. A second later they rammed into Deja, basically pushing her into the median before speeding away. The video then snapped to several still views of the same truck on regular city streets. Frowning, I sat hunched over like that would help me see better, even though the truck was tinted out and didn't have any distinct features. I watched all the way through until it disappeared into an alley and the video ended.

Sucking my teeth, I dialed Lucky's ass back up and he answered quickly like always. "Nigga, what the fuck was that? I thought you actually had something to show me!"

"My bad Bishop, that was all I could get. I'm still working on the footage from around that time. There was an accident over there that fucked up the cameras, but I swear I'll figure it out. In the meantime though, I got that information you wanted on dude's daughter. I can send that to you now if you want." I could hear clicking in the background, letting me know he was on his computer as usual, and although I was pissed off about the cameras, I wasn't going to deny the information he did have for me. Looking up at the house with a sigh, I nodded as if he could see me.

"Yeah, gone head send that shit over, and stay on top of those cameras bro, I need that shit like yesterday." I didn't even give him a chance to respond, hanging up just as Rook pulled into the driveway behind me. Before I could get out to meet him, my phone was going off with Lucky's message. I was reading over what he'd sent when Rook walked up, and I handed the phone over so he could see.

Frowning, he took it from me, taking in the picture in confusion. "Nigga, fuck you showin' me this young ass girl for? I know Deja left yo' goofy ass, but don't get on no pedo shit," he scoffed, trying to hand it back. I immediately mugged the shit out of him for saying that stupid shit, trying hard to resist the urge to punch his ass.

"Quit fuckin' playin' with me, that's Diego's daughter, fool."

"Ohhh, I was bouta say." He shrugged and nodded his understanding, finally taking a closer look. His expression

turned serious as he studied the picture and then scrolled
through her information. Lucky had included everything from
her date of birth to what school she went to and just like me,
Rook was already thinking of ways to put it to use. He'd been
wanting to go rescue Golden as soon as he discovered that
she'd left, but between finding out about King, taking care of
Aunt Milly's funeral and killing Angelo's ass, it had gotten put
off. Plus we would've been going in blind, but now we had
some leverage. I couldn't lie, as fucked up as I was, I didn't
want to harm a kid, especially when it wasn't her fault that she
was in this shit, but if it was going to lure Diego out then I
wasn't above tossing a bag over her head and throwing her in a
trunk for a little bit. That was better than what some people
got fucking around with me.

"Ayite bet, so we catching a flight tonight?" his thirsty ass
quizzed, handing the phone back to me. No doubt he was
probably ready to get on a plane right that minute and was
only saying later for my benefit. *Old pressed ass nigga.* I couldn't
even lie though, if Deja was in the clutches of a lunatic like
Diego, I would've been rushing too. I caught an attitude at how
quickly she'd entered my head unprovoked. Shaking thoughts
of her away, I shoved my phone down in my pocket and
prepared to head inside.

"Tonight is a stretch," I told him truthfully. While I understood him wanting to go out to Miami ASAP, we didn't have a
plan or anything and we were also dealing with more pressing
matters, like our snake ass pops.

"Fuck you mean a stretch? Yo' ass ain't doin' shit." Without
looking, I already knew his childish ass had his face balled up
as he followed me to the door.

"Nigga, I'm just saying *tonight* is a stretch, not that we can't
go at all," I said after ringing the bell. As big as the new house
was, I expected Knight to take all day to answer and was

surprised as fuck when the door swung open after only a second. Instead of my brother though, a flustered looking Ava answered holding Ky, who was drooling on her shoulder.

"Hey y'all, Knight's in his office." She quickly ushered us in and went to walk off, but I stopped her. I knew she'd come down to help Knight out with Blessing since everything happened. He'd already told us that sis was stuck in bed after they basically banned them from seeing Kal, and I hadn't seen her ass since. I didn't have a way with words when it came to shit like that, so I'd steered clear and since he wasn't really saying too much, I decided to pick her brain real quick.

"How's she doin'?" I nodded toward the stairs even though I was sure she knew who I was talking about, and she sighed heavily, hoisting Ky's big ass up further onto her hip.

"The same, she's at least eating a little bit, but she won't get out of bed, not even for this little guy." She sounded just as drained as she looked and I instantly felt bad. I made a mental note to ask Knight if he wanted me to take out the DCFS lady. If it would make her feel better and inevitably get them back in the hospital, then I was willing to add her to my already growing list of people that needed to die.

I didn't tell her ass that though. Instead, I gave her what felt like a sympathetic look. "Don't worry, she gone come out this shit," I assured her, even though at this point I didn't know how true that was. Her eyes glistened with tears and she shook her head.

"I hope so," she mumbled as Ky began stirring in his sleep. "Let me get him down for his nap. I'll see you guys later." I watched as she disappeared up the stairs.

"That shit crazy as fuck," Rook said, snapping me out of my thoughts with a deep sigh. We really had a lot going on and the sooner we got the shit straightened out, the better. Shaking my head, I started in the direction of Knight's office, noting how much more decorating had gotten done since the last time I'd been there.

Knight was sitting behind his desk with his phone up to his ear when we entered, and I could tell from the expression on his face that he wasn't happy about what he was hearing. A second later he hung up and let out a frustrated groan before giving us his attention.

"Everything straight?"

"Hell no, that was the fuckin' lawyer. He basically said there wasn't shit we could do regardless of Kal's condition and that we should be lucky they didn't try to remove Ky from our care too." He frowned, reclining back in his seat.

"Want me to handle that?" I offered, dropping into one of the chairs in front of his desk while Rook took the other.

"Nigga, even if you did they'd just send another one out. Killing the bitch ain't gone help." Rook shook his head at me like he disapproved, and I shrugged, unbothered. I didn't know the inner workings of that shit, but it seemed to make sense.

"If it ain't shit we can do but wait, then I'll wait. It shouldn't take long for her ass to figure out we didn't have nothing to do with that shit," Knight grumbled. "In the mean-time, we need to find Angelina, at least then maybe Blessing will somewhat get back to normal."

"I mean with Angelo gone, it won't be too much longer. Them bitches really ain't shit without that nigga. Low key, I could probably call Jules's ass right now and find out where they at. You know she's the weakest link." Rook pulled his phone out for emphasis and quickly dialed her number, putting the phone on speaker so we could hear.

Irritation clouded his face when the voicemail picked up and he tried again, getting the same results. "Nigga, you know she blocked yo' ass after you put her out yo' office." Knight said exactly what I was thinking, prompting him to hang up.

"Don't trip, I can get her ass to unblock me. While I'm working on that though, this nigga got the info on Diego's kid. We can go snatch up his daughter, trade her for Golden, and be back like we never left." Knight just stared blankly at that nigga before turning his attention to me.

"His ass serious?"

"I think so." Disbelief covered his face and I just shook my head. Wasn't no way he believed it would go down like that, but the determination in his eyes said that's exactly what he thought.

"Look, I'm going to get my wife back, it's just a matter of whether or not Bishop coming with me." Rook shrugged and stood up. "I'ma be at the crib packing, let me know what you gone do." I was still sitting there stuck as he left, and I shared a look with Knight. Now I'd have to make the impromptu trip with his ass just to make sure he got out of there alive since he wanted to act childish.

"I'll to make sure he straight. How you doin' though? Any word on Ky's condition?" I'd been treading lightly when it came to my nephew, mostly because I see the whole situation was stressing my brother out. His ass looked like a whole old man out here and a few strands of gray hair had already popped up in his beard. He leaned back and stroked his beard as he tried to figure out what he wanted to say.

"I'm fucked up, they won't even give us phone updates on Kal, and Blessing's so depressed behind that shit that she won't even fuck with Ky. On Mama's grave, when I get my hands on Angelina, I'm gone make her wish she never breathed in my direction!" he fumed, sounding like he was fighting back the urge to cry out of anger. Angelina had done so much to him in such a short amount of time that I was sure he was ready to skin her ass alive. Wherever Angelo had them hidden they were smart enough to stay inside, but I knew it wouldn't be long before she fucked up, and I couldn't wait until she did.

"Don't stress, we're definitely going to get that bitch and King's grimy ass." The mention of our father had him letting out an annoyed grunt.

"Yeah, I gotta ride back through the house and see if I can find out what all he had going on, because I'm sure fucking with Angelo wasn't the only snake shit he was on."

"Right, right," I mumbled. I was still pissed off about how King's actions were resulting in our mama's only sister having to get cremated instead of being buried next to her. Of course, he'd been into some other shit, it was just a matter of finding out what. "Well I guess I'm going to pack too so I can keep an eye on yo' knucklehead ass baby brother," I told him part of the truth as I stood and reached over to give him a pound. Really, I was going to check on Deja's ass first. Even though the immediate threat of Diego had been eliminated, I still felt like she needed some type of protection after seeing the video. With her memory back, I knew she was back to her regularly scheduled program and would for sure be at the studio, so that was my first stop.

As soon as I pulled up, my forehead immediately bunched seeing that it was closed with a big ass sign over the top that said 'Coming Soon' a fucking bridal shop. There wasn't no way Deja had sold her grandma's business when it meant so much to her. Some shit wasn't right and I skidded out of my parking spot enroute to her crib.

CHAPTER EIGHT
DEJA

After coming to terms with what my family was willing to go through to hurt me, I immediately tried to figure out a way to get my shit back. First, I went to the people who'd bought the studio from them and tried to explain what happened. Despite it making perfect sense to me, the woman and her mother looked at me like I was some random ass crazy lady despite me showing proof of who I was. Apparently, Drea had pretended to be me during the sale and although they seemed concerned about the implications of fraud, they wanted to speak with a lawyer first. I understood their worries but at the same time, that was something they'd have to take up with my conniving ass sister and her husband. How they'd get their money back when it was obvious that my family had spent it all was beyond me, but that wasn't my problem. My only concern was getting back what was rightfully mine before they started trying to remodel my shit. Next, I went to make a police report because that seemed like the next option to legitimize my claims. While the lady hadn't wanted to allow me to take pictures of their paperwork, I knew her ass wasn't going to deny the police from doing so. They'd let me file a report and said they would look into it, but I could already tell they didn't take me serious, so I was already in a bad mood when I pulled up at home, and it only grew worse seeing my baby daddy pulling in behind me.

I'd been keeping my grandmother's gun on me since I got it out of the closet and I was prepared to use it on his ass just like I'd done my family. By the time I climbed out of my car, he was already standing next to the door waiting on me with his face balled up.

"You sold the studio?" was the first thing out of his mouth, stunning the fuck out of me. I thought for sure he was there to try and find out if I'd gone through with killing the baby like I'd said or at the very least to get his car back. Anger instantly burned in my chest thinking of how he'd lied to me just like the other people in my life, and I rolled my eyes with a snort.

"Why do you even care? Don't you got a wife you need to be worrying about?" I said smartly, and I could tell the mention of Lovelie annoyed him from the way his jaw clenched, but that wasn't my problem. If he thought he was going to come questioning me about anything then he had me fucked up. When he didn't say anything, I went to walk away, but he trapped me with an arm on the top of the car.

"Just answer the question Deja, damn!"

"No, okay! My sneaky ass sister and mama sold the studio out from under my nose while I was out in buck fuck nowhere with yo' ass suffering from memory loss, and they're trying to sell my damn house too! I came home to a fuckin' open house and where they informed me that they held my signed deed," I huffed, noting the evil gleam in his eyes at my admission. No doubt he already didn't like my mama or Drea's asses after the couple of interactions he'd had with them, and finding out the type of shit they were on in my absence only made it worse. I tried to blink back the tears I felt burning my eyes as I thought about the fact that I may not be able to get the rights back to any of my shit. For some reason, despite how much I hated his ass right then, I still wanted him to embrace me, and I knew that wasn't shit but his baby. My emotions were all over the place since getting my memory back, and although I knew it was greatly due to the shit I had going on, I knew our child also played a role. It seemed like the longer I was away from Bishop the more I was being hit with bouts of crying or random anger. I wasn't even sure if that shit was normal, but I had been dealing with so much other shit that I hadn't even had time to schedule a doctor's appointment. I knew that was one of the most important things to do considering the stress I was under, and I needed to make time for that.

"So, they sold the studio out from under you and were trying to sell your crib too?" he repeated slowly, like he was trying to make sure he understood me right. Sniffling, I nodded in confirmation, unable to meet his intense stare. He scrubbed a hand down his face and looked off, still clenching his jaw tightly. I wasn't sure what I thought he was about to do, but his silence had my chest tightening. Before I could say anything else, he nodded stiffly and walked back toward his car.

"Where are you—Bishop, I already made a police report!" I called out to his back, but his gait didn't stop or get any slower and he didn't turn around. I started to follow him but he was already behind the wheel and pulling off before I could get anywhere near his car. Baffled, I watched as he sped away, unsure of how to feel. A small part of me knew exactly what he was about to do and as the realization set in, I found myself stopping. My mama and sister had lied, stolen from me, and were willing to leave me homeless and without an income just to feed their need for what they considered to be the finer things. Even when they saw how their actions had hurt me they didn't feel any remorse, and so as I watched Bishop's car disappear around the corner, I didn't feel an ounce of pity for the hell he was about to rain down on them.

A surprising calm came over me and I headed back to my car to get my things out before going into the house. Once inside, I set everything down near the door and dialed up my doctor's office to finally schedule my appointment since it was obvious my baby daddy was going to handle my lightweight. If there was one thing I knew about Bishop Grand, it was that he was going to get shit done, so I ordered me some food next and sat my ass on the couch to wait for him to return.

CHAPTER NINE
BISHOP

Before I was even off of Deja's block I was calling Lucky, letting him know to stop whatever he was doing and get me everything he could on Deja's mama and sister. Knowing that they'd used her moment of weakness to do some underhanded shit like sell her studio and try to sell her house had me beyond heated. I should've known there was a reason behind the way they were acting at the hospital and afterward. I thought it was because of me and the shit that Lovelie had been telling Drea, but clearly had everything to do with them hoes being jealous. The level of treachery had me squeezing the steering wheel until my knuckles turned white as I waited on Lucky to give me the information I'd requested. I really wanted to do them dirty and make their asses suffer, but since they were already in the process of trying to sell her house I didn't have much time. Besides that, I still needed to fly down to Miami with Rook in a few hours.

It took only a few minutes for him to run me both the mama's and Drea's addresses and I immediately recognized one but couldn't place from where. I had him send it over to me as I made my way home so I could pack a quick bag. Since I wasn't planning on having to be out there long, I wasn't bringing too much even though we still needed to do some recon.

After tossing three days' worth of clothes in a small black duffle, I sat down, still just as pissed as I'd been when I left Deja's. I figured I'd have calmed down after a while, but an hour had passed and not even cleaning my guns could take my mind off the grimy shit they'd done. I was too smart to go in guns blazing after Deja had filed a police report. They'd immediately go after her and I didn't want that. My goal was only to get back her property and ensure that they never crossed her again, and if she ended up in jail then I'd have failed miserably.

I needed more time but I was willing to settle on some help since two heads were better than one. Knight would've been preferable but with all the shit he had going on, coming to help me kill Deja's people wasn't something he could be pulled away for, so I did the next best thing and called Rook.

"Ahhh, see, I knew yo' ass was gone come through! I already got yo' ticket," he answered, talking shit as usual with his annoying ass.

"Ayite, you got that, but we got some other shit to handle before we leave so grab yo' bag and slide on me real quick." I sighed, glad that he immediately caught on with no questions asked.

"Bet, I'm on my way." He hung up quickly and a half hour later he was letting himself in my crib. I shot his goofy ass a look for just walking up in my shit, but he only shrugged before dropping onto the couch beside me. "Ayite, so what's up bro?"

"What's up is stop just walking up in my shit uninvited." I mugged him as he made himself comfortable.

Waving me off, he sucked his teeth. "Nigga, you did invite

me. Just get to the point so we can get this shit over with and make our flight," he griped dismissively, and even though I wanted to slap his ass upside the head, I let him slide since we were pressed for time.

"We need to kill Deja's mama and sister."

His jaw dropped in overexaggerated shock and he immediately shook his head. "Naw bro, yo' ass trippin' for real. Shorty ain't never gone forgive you if you kill her people. I mean, maybe her sister but her *mama?* Ain't no comin' back from no shit like that," he tried to warn, still shaking his head dramatically, and I blew out an annoyed breath before going into an explanation of why they needed to go. By the time I was finished, he looked just as pissed as I felt.

"Daaaamn, them bitches on some KG shit," he noted, and the confusion on my face had him sighing an explanation. "Nigga, KG? King Grand shit. You know, grimy, underhanded snake shit," he explained, and I just shook my head at his goofy ass.

"Man, I ain't fuckin' with you. You gone help or not?"

"Oh, for sure. They definitely gotta go behind some shit like that, but we gotta flight tonight at two, so whatever we doin' it need to be in the next couple hours." I was already way ahead of him and had been thinking of ways to handle it. Since Deja had gone to the police it seemed like it would make sense for them to just disappear. Then it would look like they'd actually committed fraud and had gone on the run.

We waited until nightfall and pulled up to the sister's house first since snatching up her and her husband would be more difficult than Deja's old ass mama. As soon as I laid eyes on the house, I immediately remembered where I knew her address from. This was where Larry's bitch ass lived, and it was crazy that I hadn't already put two and two together, but it all made sense. We'd forgotten all about his debt and the time limit we'd given him since he was the very least of our worries, but now I had even more of a reason to run up in there. I couldn't lie, the excitement that came over me knowing I was about to kill two birds with one stone had me rushing to get out.

"Ain't this that one nigga crib?" Rook quizzed as I checked to make sure my safety was off, and I grinned wickedly, confirming that it was.

"It damn sure is."

"Oh, this shit gone be good!" He nodded, rubbing his hands together gleefully before we both climbed out. Since this was going to be more serious than an ass whooping, we went to the back door instead of knocking on the front. As we walked around the side of the house, I could hear them talking loudly. Apparently, the police had stopped by to ask them about the shit Deja had reported, so they'd called the mama over to discuss their next moves. Listening to them all plot on how to get away with what they'd done had me picking up my step, and I was kicking down the back door in seconds. Their shrieks and screams led us to the living room where they had dropped down to the floor, thinking it was the police, and I chuckled as I dropped my hood.

"Damn, y'all wasn't gone try to run or shit? That's crazy! Y'all like the world's dumbest criminals!" Rook's childish ass was damn near doubled over laughing as he held his gun on them, and the shit was made even funnier by the dumb looks on their faces. For sure if they had known it was us and not the police they would've definitely run, but since they hadn't it was better for us.

"B-Bishop, man, I got y'all's money, it's in the back!" Larry tried to plead, sending Rook into another fit of laughter.

"Oh, this ain't got shit to do with that, although we would've eventually got around to offing yo' ass." Shrugging, I dropped down so that I was eye level with where he was on his knees huddled up with his wife and mother in-law. "I'm here for Deja." I grinned at their horror-stricken faces as reality set in, and before they could fix their lips to beg, I knocked them both upside the head with the butt of my gun. Seeing them slumped over, Deja's mama immediately began copping her plea.

"Listen, I was just trying to help Deja! They told me once we sold the house and studio that she'd get half the money so she could start a new life!" she lied, scooting away from me. Acting as if I believed any of that bullshit, I stood to my full height and stroked my beard thoughtfully.

"Okay, so you gone sign back over the deed?"

Her eyes lit up with hope that I was planning to extinguish momentarily. "Yes! Yes, it's actually in my purse right there! I swear I'll sign it right now if you just let me go. Y'all won't ever hear from me again!" While she continued to ramble, I reached over and picked up her big ass bingo bag where the deed sat right on top rolled up. Tossing the bag aside, I looked over the paper, noting how well she'd signed her daughter's signature before handing it off to Rook, and she followed the movement with her eyes. "Okay, so I can go now?" Her voice went up an octave and I dropped the act.

"Yeah, you bouta go with their asses," I said, knocking her out too. She slumped to the floor without even putting up a fight.

"Man, that shit was easy as hell. I hope shit in Miami go this quick," Rook mused, coming up beside me and looking down at them as they laid sprawled out. I couldn't lie, it had been much easier than I thought to get their dumb asses, but there wasn't no way it was going to be that smooth with Diego. I wasn't going to tell him that though. Instead, I agreed before we went to work tying them up and taking them out to the cars. While I loaded mine up with the mama, Rook put Drea and Larry in their own trunk. Once we had that taken care of, we set their house on fire before pulling off, and in less than an hour we'd officially gotten Deja's crib back. Now I just had to get the studio back next.

CHAPTER TEN
LOVELIE

Drea really thought we were friends and had been keeping me posted about everything going on with her trying to sell her sister's house. I couldn't lie, I enjoyed hearing the dirty details and had even sent a few buyers her way, not that anybody I associated with closely would have ever lived in that shitty house, but it was still funny nonetheless. It felt like karma coming back to bite that bitch in the ass after she stole my nigga out from under me, but I still wasn't satisfied, especially since I hadn't been getting any updates from Drea.

It was so bad that I was contemplating calling her ass, but I didn't want to seem desperate. I had Harry's ugly ass looking for the perfect opportunity to strike, but since he couldn't get too close I was still very much out of the loop when it came to Bishop and Deja. After the way we'd left things I knew I couldn't just call him up and ask how things were going, so I settled on the next best option. *Telling my daddy.*

I pulled up to my parents' home and took a minute to get into character, forcing tears out and tousling my hair so I looked like I'd crawled out of bed. I'd even tried to dress down but I didn't have anything in my closet that didn't flatter me, so I'd opted on a t-shirt and some hot pink biker shorts. Immediately, my father would know something was wrong if I wore that over because he didn't like me showing too much skin. I checked my appearance in the mirror and was pleased with the way my mascara had run down my face and how red my eyes were. Blowing myself a kiss, I got out and stumbled up to the porch just in case my daddy was watching the cameras. I rang the bell, hyping myself up as I waited for someone to answer the door, and was surprised when my mother appeared. She looked just as put together as always and her beautifully made-up face instantly turned up at the sight of me.

"Oh my lord girl, what's the matter with you!"

"It's Bishop, Mama!" I wailed, falling into her arms. Sucking her teeth, she ushered me inside and called out to my father. I allowed her to guide me to the sitting area and buried my face in her bosom once we reached the couch.

"What is wrong? Who upset my darling!" I heard my father before I saw him, but I continued clinging to my mother since my dumb ass hadn't thought of what exactly I'd say. As I thought of a good reason why I was so distressed, I cried harder and my mama decided to answer for me.

"It's that *boy*! He's been nothing but trouble since they married. I told you he was no good!" she fussed, even though I hadn't said anything besides Bishop's name, but I was still thankful for her butting in.

"Is that true? Bishop did this?" my father quizzed, like he couldn't just take her word for it, and her spine straightened. I knew she hated when he dismissed her but since she never wanted to speak up for herself, I wasn't going to either.

Sensing that he was expecting an answer from me, I finally brought my head up and just like my mother, his expression gave away how crazy I looked. "Yes! I've done nothing but be a perfect wife to him and not only hasn't he been home, but he got his little whore pregnant! Are you happy now!" Surprise washed over him at the revelation, but he quickly recovered with a scoff.

"Is that why you're over here disturbing our nightly routine, Lovelie?" His tone was accusatory and before I could stop myself, I snapped out of my act.

"What do you mean? Yes, that's why I'm here. Aren't you going to do something? Call him over here and talk to him like you did for Diego!" Anger took over and now the tears streaming down my face were from frustration. I knew first-hand how much he'd gone out of his way for my godfather's perverted ass, but he was looking at me, his own daughter, like he didn't even care. Even as I stood there begging, I might as well have had three heads. I could feel my mother pulling at my arm to rein me in but I shook her off, pissed that, as usual, she was being a coward.

"Lovelie, you watch how you talk to me!" he thundered, and despite my strong front, my heart pounded in my chest. "Not that I have to explain anything to you, but me setting up a sit down for Diego was *business*! I'd never waste resources on a marital spat, you should know that better than anyone! Now if you're having problems in your marriage, I suggest you try to figure out why he'd rather give his seed to a whore instead of you! Now if that's all." His voice returned to a normal pitch, although it was still very stern, and so was the glare he sent me and my mother before disappearing back the way he'd come.

I was still looking after him when I felt her come up behind me and place what I assumed was a comforting hand on my shoulder. "Lovelie," she said softly when I snatched away. "You have to understand that your father and I come from a different time. Men didn't meddle in other men's affairs and they certainly didn't meddle in their marriages. The biggest problem in your union is that you don't know your place. We aren't the type of women that fight and wreak havoc in our men's lives, we bring them peace and children. Give that man a son and you'll have it much easier." I didn't even try to explain to her why that wasn't going to be possible because it was obvious neither of their asses listened. If Bishop was actually fucking me, I would've been pregnant. He'd clearly given his seed to the woman he wanted to have it, but I'd be damned if I let that happen.

"Okay Mama," I sighed, barely noticing that she was guiding me to the door. I had to come to terms with the fact that this was how my mother showed her love, by giving me docile advice that didn't even work for her. She tenderly kissed my cheek before closing the door in my face, and after a few seconds of standing there I made my way back to my car. Obviously, my parents wouldn't be any help, so I was going to turn to the only person who seemed to have my back this whole time.

CHAPTER ELEVEN

ROOK

After disposing of Deja's people and changing, we made it to the airport right on time. Bishop's ass was lucky too, because if we had missed our flight fucking around with him, I would've been pissed. I wanted to look out for my girl just like his ass did, and although she'd left, I knew it was only to get that nigga Diego off our backs. Despite being irritated as fuck that she'd taken it upon herself to fix shit for us, I couldn't help being a little proud too. As terrified as she was of that nigga, she'd bossed up and tried to sacrifice herself for the family. That was some straight ride or die shit that I knew the likes of Jules would've never done. I definitely appreciated her being so selfless, but I was going to fuck her up for putting herself in danger as soon as we were in the clear.

Once we landed, the first thing on the agenda was to get some guns from somebody Lucky hooked us up with, get a room, and then immediately start recon on Diego's daughter, Estelle. From the information sheet we'd gotten on her she was only thirteen, so there couldn't have been much she had going on.

"You set up a rental?" was the first thing out of Bishop's mouth when our feet touched the sidewalk, and I had to hit him with a stale face.

"Now you know damn well I ain't do no shit like that. They be too far into a muhfucka business just to drive them snitchin' ass cars." Shaking my head, I scoped out the busy street in front of us while he burned a hole in the side of my face.

"Nigga, type of sense that make? We're over a thousand miles from home and you ain't wanna rent a car 'cause why?"

"'Cause they want too much information," I repeated. "They want your ID, social, proof of insurance, and a fuckin' credit card. Then they track where you go and all types of shit in them damn cars! I done seen a few muhfuckas get knocked messin' around with a rental."

He looked at me doubtfully. "When the fuck you ever seen some shit like that?"

"On the ID channel." Shrugging like it should've been obvious, I hoisted my bag up higher on my shoulder. "Golden's ass put me on. I'm tellin' you, that shit addictive." The thought had me missing my girl even more. It wasn't shit like coming home to her laid up in bed watching that true crime shit and eating junk food like a little psycho.

"I'ma take yo' word on it." Bishop snorted, interrupting my thoughts. "How the fuck you plan on getting around though? 'Cause it's hot as fuck out here and in a minute, I'm gone take my ass back in there, grab a rental, and leave yo' goofy ass stranded." He wasn't lying. The sun was beating our asses and even though we'd only been standing outside for less than five minutes, I could already feel my shirt beginning to stick to my body.

"Ayite, fuck it, let's just get a car, 'cause I ain't tryna get in none of these cabs." I looked at the line of awaiting cabs with my nose turned up before turning back to Bishop, who was mugging the fuck out of me. Unfazed, I nodded toward the entrance since his ass still hadn't moved. "Come on nigga, and it's going in yo' name too."

I'd only been kidding about him getting the car, but when he walked up to the counter and slapped down a credit card, I stepped aside. Bishop acted like he was one of those niggas that rode off the radar and didn't want to subscribe to things like using a social security number and building credit. The only reason he'd gotten his own crib was for privacy and so that he didn't have to be around King all the time, so to see his ass with a credit card like a real adult was...surprising, but in a good way.

It took damn near an hour for them to finally give him the keys, but since it gave us a break after being in that hell degree weather, I didn't mind. The first thing I did when we got in the truck was cut up the AC to full blast while Bishop got the directions to a decent hotel near Diego's crib. The closest we got was a few miles away, but I was willing to accept anything just to get out the damn sun until later when it was time to meet up with Lucky's people. I damn sure wasn't trying to get caught out there without a gun, and I knew Bishop felt the same.

Unfortunately, that hotel was booked solid and so were the next three we decided to call instead of wasting more time. When we finally were able to find a room, it was only one king-sized bed and Bishop was heated. I could admit it had been crazy to randomly book a flight and expect a miracle, but we'd already wasted enough time. It was mandatory that we get Golden back before Diego could hurt her, if he hadn't already. The thought alone had my eyeballs moving rapidly behind my lids and unable to settle into rest even though I was dog tired.

My sudden bout of insomnia could've also been due to Bishop's big ass lying next to me. Outside of the king bed, there was a pullout couch in the room but I refused to curl my long ass up on that shit, and since Bishop had refused too, we were sharing the bed like some little ass kids.

I just laid there resting my eyes instead of succumbing to my tiredness, but when Bishop finally woke up hours later, I did too. My anxiousness at being that close to getting Golden had me no longer sleepy as he texted the dude about where we were meeting.

The sun had finally gone down but it was still pretty warm out when we left the room, and the streets seemed even busier than they were when we'd arrived. Women were out in droves and a few had tried to shoot their shot as we left the hotel. Declining every advance, we got to our car and Bishop quickly put in the address he'd been sent. After a while of driving it was obvious we were in a different part of the city that wasn't so glamorous, and I instantly looked at my brother with a side eye. If he was concerned about how sketchy shit looked, he didn't show it. His face was just as emotionless as always as he pulled up in front of a one-level home that was separated from the others on the block by an open lot. Despite it being dark out, kids were still out running around and the few adults that were around didn't look like they gave a damn. He scoped out the house for a few seconds before nodding for me to get out.

"Come on," he said with one foot on the ground already.

"You sure you trust this nigga?" I stalled, skeptically looking around even though there didn't seem to be anything out of the ordinary that I could see.

"Yeah man, come on." Bishop waved me on, clearly irritated by my cautiousness, and after a second, I followed him up to the house. He gave three slow knocks and the door crept open, revealing a petite girl with a gun at her side. I couldn't hide my surprise at her little ass being the one we were meeting, and my forehead bunched.

"What's the magic words?" she quizzed, looking us over with narrowed eyes.

Bishop released an annoyed breath before mumbling, "Lucky 7."

A cheesy grin spread across her face and she pulled the door open wider, revealing two other girls that were slowly putting down big ass rifles. "Come on in." She stepped aside so we could enter, and I took my time stepping into the quaint living room.

"Aw hell naw! Y'all who we s'posed to be meeting?" I chuckled in disbelief. I just knew Lucky hadn't sent us to a bunch of high schoolers for the type of shit we were in search of.

"Were you expecting some big ass niggas with dreads and tattoos?" one of the girls on the couch asked smartly with her nose turned up.

"Hell yeah!"

"Well, surprise!" she mocked, spreading her arms with a smirk. "You got us. Now what you need before I get offended and change my mind?"

"Don't mind my sister, she hates gender roles," the one who let us in said, rolling her eyes, and her sister did the same, grumbling under her breath. "I'm Shayla, and these are my sisters, Riley and Ky'lee, and you're Bishop and Rook, right?" She made sure the door was locked as she correctly guessed who was who before tucking her gun in the back of her skinny jeans. I was still stuck on how young they all looked but Bishop confirmed she had it right.

"Yeah, Lucky said you're the quiet one and you're the one with all the jokes." Riley's attitude was still evident as she returned to twisting up her weed grinder and her sister Ky'lee stayed mute.

"Y'all definitely exactly how he described." Shayla chuckled with a shake of her head. "Anyway, what y'all need? We got everything from regular handguns to military grade shit, you know, Ars, machine guns, grenades." She ticked off a long list of different artillery like she was talking about ice cream flavors.

"We need some of everything. I don't wanna take no chances, and throw a couple of those grenades in just in case."

"Damn, who the fuck y'all tryna take out, Ron Desantis?" Riley's rude ass scoffed from the couch.

"Now you know we don't ask questions, Ry. If they cool with Lucky then they good peoples.... Right?" Ky'lee finally spoke, looking at Bishop to confirm.

"Of course," was all his crazy ass said, seemingly relaxing their nerves.

"Gone head take em' up, Shay." Riley nudged her head toward the back and Shayla waved for us to follow her. By now I was no longer concerned, I was intrigued more than anything and I made a mental note to ask Lucky about the group of sisters. They definitely had to have a crazy ass back story.

Shayla was obviously the spokesperson of the group. She rambled about all types of shit as she led us through the house that looked way better on the inside than outside. You could tell they were getting money, and I couldn't help but wonder why they were still living in the heart of the hood when they were clearly holding. When we reached the back hall, she pulled down one of those attic strings and some stairs came down. We followed her up and entered what looked like a department store for guns. Just like she'd said, they had everything, and she pulled out a black duffle bag and began loading it down with a variety of guns and ammo.

By the time we left we had more than enough to complete our mission. Considering that Diego was an arm's dealer, there was probably no limit to the type of shit he could get his hands on, but we were hoping that with the element of surprise plus the shit the girls had armed us with, we'd be able to walk away from this shit with Golden in tow.

CHAPTER TWELVE

GOLDEN

I swallowed the vomit that had managed to come up in my throat as Diego rolled off of me, and hurriedly wiped my tears. Since I'd returned, he made sure to reclaim my body, as he called it. For some reason he thought he could wipe away any traces of Rook, but he was clearly living in a land of delusion. Rook was engrained in every part of me down to my soul, so there was no cleansing my body of him. Which was why I was even there in the first place. I'd only returned to stop his assault on my family, and I was sure he knew that, but what he didn't know was that I also planned to kill him.

"That was wonderful as always, my love," he panted happily, wiping sweat from his forehead like he'd really put in work. Every time he touched me I felt disgusting, like I needed to bathe in a tub of bleach and ammonia. It didn't help that his old man cologne always clung to my skin afterward. I felt him reaching for me and quickly slid away, climbing out of bed and pulling the sheet along with me. "Where are you going?"

The question had my eyes rolling into my head because he knew better than anybody the type of leash he had on me, so there were only so many places I could go within the walls of his house. "To shower," I said dryly, hoping that he wouldn't ask me anything else.

"Want me to join you?" His tone lowered suggestively and once again, vomit threatened to erupt.

"No, I need to hurry so I can have breakfast with Estelle." I stood frozen, basically waiting on his permission to shower alone, which was crazy as hell. I didn't even realize I was holding my breath until I heard him grunting as he struggled out of bed. Bringing up his daughter had been strategic on my part, but I should've known Diego didn't give a damn about anything concerning her.

I tried to race to the bathroom before he could reach me, but I barely made it to the door before he grabbed me roughly by the back of the neck. "You think you're too good to take a shower with your husband, *puta!*" he growled in my ear before slamming my head into the wall, stunning me. Stars danced around my head as he berated me, and I fought hard not to pass out. "You think that nigga is coming for you, but he's not, and the sooner you understand that there's no getting out of this marriage, the better!"

A knock at the door stopped him from hitting me again, but he didn't release his hold on my neck. I was immediately grateful for the interruption since it gave me some relief, even though his grip was still tight enough that it hurt but didn't obstruct me from breathing.

"Boss!" I recognized his head of security Ramon's voice right away, as did he.

"*What!*"

"Something needs your attention." Groaning, Diego slung me to the floor and stormed over to the door, swinging it open despite being completely naked.

"This better be important!" he hissed, trying to block

Ramon's view of me, but the man was already focusing on the floor in an effort to avoid looking at his boss's flabby body. Whatever he told him was in such a low tone that I couldn't hear what was being said, but it must've been important because Diego cursed and told him he'd be down immediately. He ignored me as he came back into the room and passed where I was still sitting on the floor. I frowned at the fact that he had yet to remove the condom. Just as the thought crossed my mind, he pulled it off, tossing it in the trash before disappearing into the closet. He emerged a few moments later fully dressed like he hadn't just literally rolled out of bed. *Nasty ass!*

"We'll finish this when I get back. *Don't* try anything stupid," he warned evenly before leaving the room, and I finally released the breath I'd been holding and picked myself up off the floor. My head was pounding and I stumbled as a wave of dizziness hit me. It took me a minute to get my bearings but when I did, I went straight to the bathroom, holding myself up with the wall along the way. At this point, the only thing that was keeping me going was knowing that I'd be the one with the last laugh in the end. Between the things he'd done to me in the past and the recent attack on me and my family, he deserved everything that was coming to him.

By the time I got out of the shower, I could feel the knot growing on the side of my head. The spot was so tender that I elected to wear my naturally curly hair down, and I couldn't help smiling as I thought of how much Rook liked it that way. I already missed him so much that sometimes it brought me to tears, but I couldn't keep running and I couldn't allow him and his family to fight this battle for me. I was the only one that could put an end to Diego, and I planned to do just that so I could go home to my man.

I made my way downstairs and was surprised to see Estelle at the table eating a bowl of cereal in her pajamas. It was still early so I hadn't been expecting to see her up already. Despite the dull ache in my head, I smiled. She had nothing to do with her father's insanity, which I was assuming was in great part due to her mother. Upon my return, she was excited to see me, even going so far as to give me a hug. I could only imagine how things had been around there as a growing girl with no other women around besides the staff. She'd immediately clung to my hip and had been doing so since, if she wasn't away at school or practice or any of the things Diego had her signed up for in an effort to keep her out of his face.

"What you doin' up so early, honey?"

"I was hungry." She shrugged, shoveling more cereal into her mouth.

"You all ready for school? You got clothes out and everything?" I made small talk as I went about starting the Keurig in hopes that coffee would perk me up. When she didn't immediately answer, I stopped what I was doing and looked over my shoulder to see her staring at me blankly.

"I'm almost fourteen, Angel," she huffed, and I couldn't help but chuckle.

"Well excuse me, miss thing!" I snapped my fingers in a zig zag, making her snicker even as she rolled her eyes. She had definitely grown up on me, but it was hard to differentiate the teen from the little girl I met years ago. It had only been a couple of days and I could already see how much more mature she was.

Our laughter died down and I went back to making my coffee as silence fell over us. Honestly, I was just about to ask her what she had planned for the day when she cleared her throat and said, "I heard you and my daddy earlier." Her statement had me frozen for a couple of reasons as I tried to figure out how I was going to respond. For one, I wasn't exactly sure what she had heard. I only ever cried silently when her father was forcing himself on me, but he always went out of his way to moan loudly like it was that good. For some reason, I was more ashamed of her possibly hearing that than the fight we had that morning.

"Huh?" I feigned confusion to buy myself some time, and she groaned lowly.

"I said I heard you and my daddy earlier... I know that's why you left before 'cause he hits you, right?" My heart dropped at the revelation, and I blinked back tears. She was clearly much more intuitive than I'd given her credit for, because I never imagined that she knew about her father's abuse. "If he does stuff like that, why did you come back?" The questions kept coming and I had no clue how to answer them in a way that she would understand. Dropping my head, I released a deep sigh.

"I, um, I'm sorry you heard that, Estelle. It's definitely not something I ever wanted you to know about, because I don't want you to think it's okay for a man to treat a woman like that but sometimes, people have their own reasons for staying in bad situations. I'm not saying it's right, but sometimes things happen that we don't have control over and we have to do what's best in those situations," I stuttered as I tried to inform her without too many details. As much as I hated Diego's ugly ass, I didn't want my feelings to affect the way she felt about him. I didn't know what to expect, but I was surprised when she released an annoyed grunt.

"Ugh, you don't have to make excuses for him, Angel, I know he's a monster. He's the reason I can't see my mom. What kind of person beats up women and won't let their kid see their own mama?" I hadn't thought about Estelle's mama much since she'd virtually disappeared. I always thought she just left because of Diego's bullshit, but it hadn't crossed my mind that he was actively keeping her away from the little girl.

By now I was facing her and the disgruntled expression she wore only further proved how much she meant everything she was saying. Selfishly, I hadn't thought about what would happen to her once I killed Diego. I couldn't see past me running off into the sunset with Rook, but to know her mother was out there somewhere probably actively trying to get to her had me thinking I should hold off.

"Estelle!" Diego's head maid, Marisol, appeared in the doorway, making us both jump. She continued speaking but turned her stern gaze on me. "You should be getting prepared for school. Rueben is bringing the car around." Without hesitation, Estelle jumped to do what the woman said, leaving us alone. I was almost sure Marisol had heard our conversation, or at least part of it by the way she stood staring at me, but since I'd returned her ass always watched me. She was one of the newer staff members that Diego must've hired in my absence, and I didn't like her ass at all. Obviously, she didn't care for me much either. She along with the twenty-plus armed guards that Diego had scattered about the house kept a watchful eye on both me and Estelle, and if by chance I tried to escape again, I was sure she'd be the first to snitch.

"Can I help you?" I asked with a curled lip when she continued to stand there, and the weird bitch smirked.

"I don't know what you *think* you're doing, but putting a wedge between them won't help you and if you continue with your foolery, I'll make sure Señor finds out."

I didn't know why she thought her threat would scare me when Diego already put his hands on me whenever the wind blew wrong, but I was far from afraid of her. If it wasn't for the fact that beating her ass might cause me to be further locked down, then I would've dragged her all over the kitchen, but instead I just waved her off.

"Girl, if you don't get the fuck out my face and go find

something to sweep or dust," I scoffed. Rolling my eyes, I turned my back to her and returned to making my coffee unfazed, and after a few seconds she disappeared back to wherever she had just come from. I could only hope she didn't go running her mouth and possibly ruin the trust I was building with Diego, or I'd have to put my plan in motion much sooner than expected.

CHAPTER THIRTEEN
ROOK

We'd spent the last couple of days learning Estelle's schedule, and it was crazy how many activities that nigga had her in. It was like he was trying to keep her ass out the house and out of his face because she was always being carted off somewhere. In just two days I'd seen her with a cello case, a dance bag, and a damn bow and arrow. A member of Diego's staff was never too far behind and despite having scoped out their house multiple times, we had yet to get a glimpse of Golden. No doubt he had her locked away for fear that she'd try to run again, but that was the least of his worries, because I was going to get her this time.

Bishop had been smart to get explosives from the girls because we used a couple to blow up his warehouse where he kept a majority of his shit. Since he was in the business of weapons, we knew he'd assume that it was due to the carelessness of his men, and it seemed to do the trick, because he'd killed every one of them that were there when it happened. While he scrambled to figure that shit out, we were going to swoop in and fuck his head up even more.

At exactly a quarter to three, we followed the two guards that picked up Estelle from school. Like clockwork, they stopped at the same restaurant to pick up her favorite smoothie and I followed the passenger inside. I waited while he placed his order and received it before trailing him back to the truck.

"Excuse me, you got some change you can spare?" I'd dressed the part of a homeless person so it was no surprise that he frowned at me like I wasn't shit, shaking his head as he opened the door with his free hand. I used that moment to tuck my gun into his side, shocking him.

Bishop popped up on the other side, jumping into the backseat and holding the driver at gunpoint at the same time.

"Get yo' rude ass in the back, nigga!" I huffed, taking the weapon off his hip before forcing him in next to Bishop, who'd unarmed the driver. Jumping into the passenger seat, I directed him to a cut we'd discovered the first day we arrived. "Ayite, now get out and don't try no weird shit," I told him once he'd parked, and he did as he was told, slowly reaching for the handle while he held his other hand in the air.

Bishop and his partner got out also, leaving their door open as they met us around the front of the truck. "Ayite, take that shit off, but keep the shoes, them muhfuckas way too small," I demanded, waving my gun to prompt them. Hesitantly, they both began stripping out of their suits and speaking Spanish rapidly in a low tone. I instantly picked up on the fact that they were praying as they realized they were probably going to die. That was probably the reason why the driver decided to take his chances and as his pants fell around his ankles, he went for a small handgun he had hidden and Bishop wasted no time shooting his ass in the head.

"Nigga, what the fuck!" I grilled him as the man's body

dropped. "You gone get blood all over the suit!" Pissed off, I went ahead and shot the other man since he had already taken everything off and had begun begging.

"You worried about blood when his ass was bouta blow yo' head off yo' shoulders." He mugged me right back, tossing the suit he was holding over to me. "Just take this one, ol' crybaby ass nigga!"

If his ass thought I was going to decline he had me fucked up, because I damn sure snatched that shit and started throwing it on while he went to get the rest of the driver's clothes off of him. Ten minutes later, we'd thrown the men in one of the huge dumpsters and were headed to Estelle's school. When we pulled up it wasn't very many kids there anymore since we were a few minutes late, but we immediately spotted her talking to another little girl as she held on to what looked like a violin case.

"Gone head, go get her." Bishop nodded from the driver's seat and I narrowed my eyes at his ass.

"Why you can't go?" I quizzed, annoyed. I didn't know shit about kids and I damn sure didn't know shit about little girls.

"'Cause you bout to, and make sure you take the smoothie." His bitch ass dismissed me, and instead of wasting time arguing with him, I snatched up the smoothie and got out, calling him a bitch under my breath. I approached the two girls, shaking my head inwardly, and their conversation ceased immediately. They sized me up, probably wondering what the fuck my grown ass was doing there when they'd never seen me before.

"Estelle, I'm Brian, I'm here to pick you up," I said, coming up with a name on the fly as I held her smoothie out for her. Skeptically, she looked from me to the cup and then over to the truck.

"Where's Rueben and Antonio?" she wanted to know, and while I admired her questioning shit, I was still irritated as fuck by it at the same time.

"They had to handle some shit—some *things* for your father, but he sent us instead. They even let me know to stop and get your favorite strawberry banana smoothie." My slip up had the friend giggling, but I kept my attention on Estelle, who still didn't seem convinced, offering her a small smile. "Listen, you don't want to be late for practice do you? We're already running behind." I followed up by checking the time on my watch and realized I'd already been standing out there a good five minutes.

"Go ahead Stelle, you know how Ms. Arturo is when you're even a minute late," her friend jumped in with a shrug. I guess they both had the same instructor, which worked out great for me because Estelle relaxed slightly and took the drink with a roll of her eyes.

"True, I'll see you later, Rita." I couldn't help frowning at the girl's name as Estelle headed toward the car, but I left it alone and grabbed Estelle's book bag and violin case. That must've been something else that wasn't normal, because she looked at me crazy as hell and put up a little struggle at first.

Bishop barely let us get in the truck good before he was swerving out into traffic, and I shot his wild ass a look before checking to make sure Estelle wasn't alarmed. As expected, her inquisitive ass was already looking at him crazy as she sipped her drink.

"This isn't the way to Ms. Arturo's," she noted, but there wasn't any concern in her voice.

"Just chill lil' mama, this a shortcut."

There was a long pause before she spoke again, still in the same even tone as before. "Is that blood on your shirt?" My head immediately snapped in Bishop's direction, and I noticed the small spot of blood on the collar of his shirt. Groaning lowly, I prepared to pull my gun out if she started screaming or acting crazy, even though I'd been trying to avoid that. The last thing I needed was a terrified teenager in the car in broad daylight.

"Yeah, I, uh, cut myself shaving," Bishop stumbled over the lie and avoided her eyes in the rearview.

"Y'all aren't really my drivers, huh?" I couldn't lie, I was stunned. I thought for sure she'd be hysterical at the realization, crying even, but she just continued to sit in the same spot seemingly unbothered as she awaited our answer. My first instinct was to lie, but I decided against it. Estelle had already saw right through me from the minute I walked up to her, so it seemed pointless to keep trying to deceive her.

"Naw, we're not—"

"Nigga!" Bishop snapped, glaring my way, but I continued ignoring his ass.

"We're not your drivers, we're actually here for Golden... You probably know her as Angel though." I'd turned around in my seat to address her and I immediately noticed the recognition at her name, even though she remained silent. "I don't know what you think the situation is with her and your father, but—"

"I know she doesn't wanna be there," she mumbled, looking away. I wanted to ask how exactly she knew that but I figured she was old enough to see and hear plenty of things that went on in that house, in addition to the fact that she was obviously smart. "I'm not gonna die, am I?"

"Naw," Bishop answered before I could, catching her eye in the rearview. "We don't do shit like that." We'd never fully discussed what we'd do with her if things went bad, but I couldn't lie and say I wasn't relieved that his mean ass wasn't trying to kill her. Now her father was a different story. I was going to make sure I did his old perverted ass dirty, I just hoped she had a distant relative or something to get her once he was no longer in the land of the living.

She didn't look like she believed him and I could understand why. Not only was Bishop's demeanor intimidating but he was tall as fuck too. He probably looked like the boogeyman to her, but she showed no fear, only resoluteness, which was both sad and scary as hell at the same time.

"On my dead mama, we won't hurt you," I promised, ignoring Bishop's stare. He hated when I said that, and I'd toned it down a lot but the situation called for it. What type of nigga would lie on their dead mother? It seemed to do the trick though, because she didn't ask any more questions. Since we couldn't take any chances by bringing her back to the busy ass hotel we were staying in, we hit up the trigger triplets and asked for a favor. They weren't going to find out what that favor was exactly until we got there though.

We went and switched cars before heading their way just in case Diego had a tracker installed. When we pulled up the block was just as lively as it had been the last time, and I said a silent prayer that shorty didn't try anything stupid. I climbed out and hurried to her door. The child safety lock prevented her from running away but even as I let her out, she didn't take off like I feared she would. I still kept a hand on her shoulder as we went up the walkway with Bishop right behind us.

Using the same coded knock as before, I stood on their stoop, ignoring the lust-filled gazes from the few neighbors that were out. I was about to knock again when the door swung open, and Shayla appeared, smiling, until her eyes landed on Estelle.

"Oh hell naw! Is this your favor, 'cause if it is, I take back what I said about helping y'all out." She was already shaking her head and while initially I was thinking about how glad I was that she was the one to open the door, the look on her face had me rethinking that shit. "What the fuck y'all doin' with a kid?"

I was instantly vexed by her question and I sighed heavily. "Just let us in, and we'll explain. You're drawing too much attention out here."

"*I'm* drawing too much attention when y'all the ones who pulled up with a whole ass kid to my house?" Her nose wrinkled even more.

"Look, just let us in," Bishop grit, ushering Estelle forward as Shayla huffed and puffed. The commotion summoned her mean ass sister from the back and she instantly started fussing.

"Whose kid y'all done stole? See, I knew I should've followed my first mind and not fucked with y'all!" Riley scoffed, eyeing Estelle.

"Maaan listen, it's a long story how we got her, but what's important is that we need to lay low here with her for a little bit." Horror crossed their faces and I couldn't hide my annoyance. I was getting tired of explaining myself and I'd used up the last bit of patience I had on Estelle by now. I guess Bishop had also because before I could speak, he cut in.

"She's leverage to get this nigga's wife back. Now either you gone watch her and keep her safe or we gone take our chances toting her around with us while we negotiate with her pops, Diego Cortez."

"Oh, this shit just keeps getting better and better!" Riley grumbled, shaking her head.

"Y'all tryna go up against Diego? No wonder you wanted so much stuff." Shayla sighed deeply and rubbed her temples. "Ok fine, we'll keep her but—"

"Bitch, what! I ain't sign up for this shit!"

"It's cool Ry, we can keep her for a few." Shayla shushed her sister and I briefly wondered if it'd be wise to leave the girl, but we didn't have much of a choice.

"We'll be right back," I promised both the sisters and Estelle before Bishop and I left to get things set up.

CHAPTER FOURTEEN

GOLDEN

It was the early evening, so the house was pretty quiet since Diego was out and Estelle was at her violin lesson. I appreciated the time alone because it gave me the opportunity to snoop. Using a tiny screwdriver and a nail file, I broke into Diego's home office and shut the door behind me just in case Marisol was still lurking. The first place I went looking was in his desk. I wasn't exactly sure what I was trying to find but I was hoping he had something on Estelle's mother in there. I came up empty, only finding business-related things in and on his desk, and I leaned back in his chair as I tried to think of where he'd hide some shit that he didn't want to be found.

Seeing a small safe on his bookshelf, I immediately shook my head. I didn't know why he'd have that right out in the open, but I hurried over to it. To my surprise, it wasn't locked like I expected and I was able to just open the door. Inside were papers from Estelle's birth certificate to immunization papers, and I quickly zeroed in on her mother's name. It wasn't much but it was something, and I quickly tucked it into my mental

Rolodex before putting everything back and closing it back so it didn't look messed with. Once I was done, I slipped back out the same way I'd come in and it was just in time, because moments later Diego was walking through the door. I played it off like I was heading toward the kitchen as he stood in the foyer with his phone pressed up to his ear. For some reason, it felt like he knew I'd been doing something I wasn't supposed to, eyeing me until I disappeared around the corner.

As soon as I was out of his eyesight I breathed a sigh of relief. I could only hope that he went about his business and didn't come fucking with me. Since the morning that his guard came and interrupted his assault on me, he'd been preoccupied. He didn't talk much around me but from what I could gather, he'd lost some of his merchandise and was desperately trying to smooth things over with any of his clients that were effected. I could only hope that one of them decided to kill his ass, but then there was a chance they'd fuck around and kill me and Estelle too. I took my time getting some water, not wanting to venture back out while he was still in the hall. Unfortunately, I heard his voice approaching and rolled my eyes.

"Angel, get dressed, we have dinner plans." He strolled in, not even bothering to greet me before making his demand with Marisol on his heels. "And make sure it's presentable, I don't want to be embarrassed." With his order given, he was gone again, leaving me alone, and I mocked him behind his back. The last thing I wanted to do was go with him anywhere let alone to dinner with him and any of his friends, but I wasn't going to tell him that.

I finished my water and made my way upstairs to do what he'd said. Looking through my closet, I quickly decided on a black Valentino, body con dress that reached just above my knees with a pair of black red bottoms. Since he'd made it seem like I should get ready right away, I went ahead and got in the shower again. While I washed up I tried to think of a way to get in contact with Estelle's mother. Diego had removed any means of me contacting anyone when he brought me there, including my phone, computers, and laptops. Hell, Estelle didn't even have a cellphone, which was unusual considering her age, but considering how controlling he was it made sense that he'd limit her social interactions as well.

I still hadn't come up with a way to find this woman by the time I got out the shower or even after sitting down to put my hair in a sleek bun. I finally figured that if worse came to worse, I'd have to take the girl with me because it wasn't too much more of her father I could stomach. Diego didn't enter the room until I was completely ready and spraying on my Tom Ford perfume. He looked at me in approval and lust danced in his eyes, but he thankfully carried his ass on in the bathroom so he could get ready himself. I silently hoped he didn't take long because it wasn't very comfortable sitting in that stuffy ass dress.

I decided against makeup, opting to just put on some tinted lip gloss. I was putting on my jewelry when Diego came out followed by a cloud of steam. "We'll be leaving once I'm dressed," he said absentmindedly as he headed toward his walk-in closet. When he came back out he was fully dressed in a black suit that I was sure he'd decided on so we could match. It seemed like he was trying really hard to impress whoever we were meeting, and I wondered why. I knew I couldn't ask him since he liked to keep me out of the loop, but I was going to make sure to listen hard during dinner. I wasn't convinced that anyone who associated with Diego would help me if they could, but the information may come in handy.

It wasn't long after that when we left and to my surprise, Diego decided to drive himself. I was already scheming in my mind about how I could use this to my advantage as he drove. We pulled up to a French restaurant and he handed off the keys to valet after helping me out onto the sidewalk. I tried to discreetly remove my hand from his sweaty one but he squeezed it tightly and gave me a warning look, which I knew all too well. He was basically telling me to stop before he beat my ass. Grinding my teeth, I allowed him to walk me inside like a child.

"Hi, welcome to Amour! Party of two?" the hostess greeted, picking up a couple of menus for us.

"Actually, we're meeting someone, the reservation should be under the name Cambridge," Diego said, looking around the restaurant.

"Oh ok, well follow me." The girl continued smiling as if she was trying to flirt. I wished her ass would've attracted his attention and took him off my hands, but that wasn't likely with the way he was ignoring her. She led us to a table in the back and I couldn't hide my surprise at seeing a beautiful girl at the table we stopped at. I hadn't been expecting a woman let alone one that looked about my age. She was completely glammed up in a sequin black dress with her hair in beautiful Kardashian-like curls. Upon seeing us, she stood to greet us with a wide smile, revealing a gorgeous set of teeth.

"Diego," she breathed, reaching out to shake his hand, and he damn near blushed as he instead lifted it for a kiss.

"Shayla, you're as beautiful as always."

"Aww, thank you," she beamed before setting her eyes on me. "And who's this lovely creature?" Diego ushered me forward like he was at show and tell.

"This is my wife, Angel. Angel, this is Shayla." He made the introductions and I shook her hand before we all took our seats. It only took us a few minutes to order and although I really wasn't hungry, I made sure to get the most expensive thing on the menu. Since Diego was trying to impress, he didn't object like he normally would have.

Once the waitress scampered off to fill our orders they began to speak about business like I wasn't even there. I didn't know how dinners went between criminals but I figured they'd wait until the food came at least. I couldn't even follow along with anything they were saying because they were obviously speaking in code. There wasn't much I could pick up on but when they said anything direct line like guns or money, I listened closely.

Apparently, Diego needed guns from her to fulfill orders and he was offering her a percentage of the sales if she agreed to give them to him. They went around in circles until our food came out, but by then I needed to use the restroom. At least that's what I told him. I was really hoping I could catch a woman in the bathroom who'd allow me to use her phone. I excused myself, gaining a look from Diego, but I gave him a reassuring smile and strutted to the bathroom, rolling my eyes once my back was to him.

Unfortunately, there wasn't a soul in the spacious bathroom, instantly sinking my spirits. Sighing, I leaned against the sink and dropped my head just as the door swung open. Shayla stepped in and immediately moved next to me with a serious expression on her face. I straightened my spine, unsure of what she was doing but wanting to be prepared if she came out the side of her neck at me. To my surprise, she broke out into a grin as soon as she stopped next to me.

"Girl! That nigga don't never shut up! I almost had to run to get away from him." She cackled, and I looked at her confused. That definitely wasn't what I was expecting to hear and I'm sure it showed on my face because she began cracking up laughing. "You seem confused girl, but Rook sent me."

"What—how?" My eyes bucked and I almost choked on my spit as she laughed harder.

Shrugging, she handed me her phone out of her clutch and checked her makeup in the mirror. "We have a mutual friend that sent him my way when he came out here on this blank ass mission, but don't worry, with me and my sister's help, you'll be back in Chicago ASAP. Go ahead, call that nigga before he lose his damn mind," she urged, and I did so cautiously. As the phone trilled in my ear, I kept an eye on her because I wasn't sure if this was even real, but the minute Rook's voice came over the line, my heart swelled.

"Hello, Shayla?"

"Rook, it's me." My voice took on a much softer tone and I was damn near on the verge of tears. It felt like it had been months since I'd heard his voice and it made me realize just how much I missed him.

"Daaaamn! Shayla really came through, bro! What's up G? You okay?"

Concern laced his tone and I tried to swallow the lump in my throat. I didn't want to piss him off by saying any of the things that Diego had done, so instead I said, "I-I'm okay, but what are you doing? You guys have too much going on to be trying to get me and have Diego waging war on you!" I whispered harshly, remembering the reason I'd decided to take on this mission in the first place.

"Don't worry about that. We're taking care of everything, just go back out there and act natural." My heart pounded in my ears, unsure of what was about to take place but still I agreed, telling him I loved him before handing the phone over to Shayla.

"Okay, you need to get back before he gets suspicious, girl." She tucked her phone away and shooed me out with a smile. The fact that she was calm, cool, and collected made me feel a little better about whatever they had planned. Nodding, I took a deep breath and returned to the table where it was obvious that Diego wasn't pleased. I'd probably only been gone less than five minutes, but he had his face twisted in a scowl like I'd dipped out on him. As soon as I took my seat, he grabbed my thigh beneath the table, pressing his nails into me.

"Whew! That wine!" Shayla returned before he could verbally chastise me and his demeanor instantly changed. *Bastard!*

"It is good wine," he mused, removing his hand from my body. "Anyway, what were we discussing?"

"Oh yes, we were talking about how you're going to let Angel here go if you want your daughter returned safely." It took him a minute to catch on to what she was saying because he was still eating his soup and instantly began choking once it registered in his brain. Even though Rook had just told me it was about to go down, I wasn't expecting it to be at the dinner table and I damn sure wasn't expecting for Estelle to somehow be involved. My breathing hitched in my throat as Diego finally found his voice.

"You what!"

"*I said*, if you want your daughter back then you need to let Angel go," Shayla repeated like she was annoyed to have to do so, and I instinctively tensed, ready for Diego to explode, but it never happened.

"Shayla, I really expected for you to be smarter than this. You know better than anyone the type of connections I have." His anger was evident by how red his face was as he coughed, still trying to recover from choking earlier.

"No, you should be smarter than to doubt me and my connections." She smirked, winking at a waitress that was walking past. I didn't think anything of it, but Diego's eyes bucked as he followed her line of vision, growing more upset.

Suddenly, his breathing picked up and he grabbed at his chest through his clothes.

"What did you do, you little bitch!" he wheezed, making her smile grow wider.

"Girl, you better act like your life depends on it," she whispered before jumping from her seat. "Oh my god, he's having a heart attack!" While she continued to scream and draw attention to us, I grabbed ahold of Diego as if I was trying to help him when really I wanted to smile in his face. As he slid from his chair, he grabbed ahold of my wrist tightly, bringing tears to my eyes that aided in my act.

A few people rushed over trying to help him as others shouted for someone to call an ambulance. By the time one of the patrons began CPR though, I could already tell it was too late for that to work. Diego died on a restaurant floor and I was finally free.

CHAPTER FIFTEEN
KNIGHT

I 'd finally figured out a way to keep up with Kal without going to jail for trespassing, and while I thought it would get Blessing out of bed, all she did was lay there watching him on camera. I had my lawyer look into a few of the nurses on his floor and we picked the one most likely to take some money for planting a nanny cam in the room. She'd done a good job placing it in direct view of his bed so we could see him at all times and see what any of the doctors and other nurses were doing to him. We'd even caught the DCFS lady up there once, but she wasn't saying anything to make us feel as if she was closing her case anytime soon.

Unfortunately, there wasn't anything the lawyer could do about fighting them on the shit. We had to just wait and see how shit played out. In the meantime, I was looking into King's dealings, starting with his house. While my brothers were off playing superheroes, I was scouting through any paperwork I could find to inform me of why King had gone off the deep end. It couldn't have just been about money, because even without our unions we were making plenty. His ass was into something else and I was going to find out, then find him.

I also had some people looking into Angelina's whereabouts. If the bitch thought she was just going to hurt my family and live to tell the story, she was crazier than I thought. Angelo had done a good job of hiding her but with as many people as I had looking, it was only a matter of time.

I entered my parents' home for the second day in a row and bypassed my dad's office since I'd already thoroughly searched it. There hadn't been much there and I assumed that was because he'd taken anything that made him look bad with him. I headed upstairs to their bedroom, this time noting that even though it had been months since my mom had passed that it still smelled like her. Looking around, I figured I'd start on his side of the bed but there wasn't much in his side table but some cash, a box of cigars and a notepad that only had old debts listed. I still pocketed it just in case it was vital and moved on to the closet. My mother's side was full as if she was coming back and only on vacation somewhere, causing me to finger a few items, thinking about her as I did. I'd pushed the hurt from her death to the far recesses of my mind since we'd been getting hit with bullshit on a consistent basis since she'd died, but I couldn't help wishing she was there. She'd know exactly what to do about every situation we were in at the moment. I had hoped that she'd given all of us the same abilities, but that was far from the truth. A wave of sadness hit me and I forced myself to get back to the task at hand. Looking at my pops's side, I started with the boxes on his shelf. That nigga had more clothes, shoes, hats, and accessories than anybody I knew, even more than my mama did. I didn't even attempt to look through his shit in an organized manner. I was tossing shit and getting pissed off every time I came up empty handed.

When I'd gone through everything, I resorted to looking through the pockets of his suits. As I pushed each one aside the wall became more visible and I could barely make out the edges of a wall safe.

"This muthafucka here." I sighed, stumped. The only safe we were aware of was the one in the basement, and yet he'd had another hidden from us for God knows how long. Aggravated, I went through the motions of guessing his combination, trying everything from his mama's birthday down to Rook's and none of them were right. Sitting down on the floor, I racked my brain trying to think of what his snake ass would use for something that none of us knew about. After a while I tried my parent's anniversary date, then their wedding date, and on a whim I typed in the day my mother died, cursing under my breath when that bitch popped open.

Inside were all types of papers, from life insurance policies upward of a million on each of us but not him. I saw forged power of attorney papers and offshore account documents. Stupefied, I shook my head as more and more of my father's dirt slapped me in the face. When I came across a police file naming him and Angelo the head of a sex trafficking ring, I was ready to explode. I'd told his ass I didn't want to have any involvement in that shit and he'd still gone and tied our family's name to it. Although there wasn't anything in there mentioning me or my brothers, I knew the police could and would rope us into that shit. Seeing that had me not even wanting to continue, but I was sure there was more I needed to be informed about. Literally all of King's skeletons were falling out of the closet and the more I learned the more I was ready to kill him. Finally reaching the bottom of the pile, a green leather notebook sat nestled in the very back of the safe and I realized quickly that it was a journal. My mother's journal. The fact that he had it locked away filled my chest with dread. As grimy as King was, I couldn't imagine that my mama, his wife, would be on the receiving end, then again, he had gone so far as to plan the demise of his own grandkids with the De'Leons.

Instead of reading through months or years of her private thoughts, I skipped to the last entry and noted that the date was right before she went on hospice. She'd become too sick to even keep any food down and was incontinent. I remembered her being so embarrassed about the shit that she couldn't even face any of us when she had an accident. It was hard to watch her decline and knowing that she felt like her journal was her only outlet made me feel like shit. She talked about how she knew my pops was fucking her nurse every chance he got, and I vowed to find and kill that bitch just off the strength. She'd kept it from us how bad things had gotten in their marriage, wanting to keep a brave face, but they'd been going through it for years according to her, even as far back as before she'd gotten pregnant with Bishop. They'd been doing tit for tat cheating and having affairs, but she said once she found out she was pregnant she put an end to hers and attempted to save their marriage and it had worked for a while; that's how she ended up with Rook. For some reason, after Rook was born my pops decided he wanted a paternity test on all of us and it was revealed that Bishop wasn't his. I'd always thought their rift was because of how much Bishop clung to our OG but obviously, it was much more than that.

I sat frozen, unable to continue as I tried to work through what the fuck I'd just read. I didn't even know if I could repeat the shit out loud to even clue my brothers in on it. How the fuck could I tell my little brother that the nigga he'd been raised by wasn't his father? Even though we were only recently finding out how fucked up King truly was, he'd still been an important figure in our lives. I knew right then that I wasn't going to tell Bishop or Rook about it and I didn't need to, because they'd never find out from anybody else.

Gathering up the papers and the journal, I started for the door. I'd already been there two whole hours and knew Ava was probably ready for a break, but first I was going to go over the financial records I'd found with my lawyer. I had to make sure me and my brothers weren't the target of an investigation and also find out if King had been anywhere near his overseas accounts. I was on his head and anybody associated with him.

An hour later I walked through the restaurant, making sure everything was running smoothly before I headed to the trucking company and then the club. I'd been checking the time on my watch every few minutes to make sure that Ava hadn't called since I was supposed to be going straight home to give her a break. I felt fucked up leaving her to handle everything but at the same time, it was easier to deal with something I was used to, like business, than to deal with a depressed Blessing and a baby that was missing his mama and his twin. Things had already been strained between Blessing and me, but now with the added stress of Kal and her basically giving up on life due to the case against us, I wasn't sure how to even talk to her let alone be there in her time of need. I could only pray that once Kal was in the clear and we put an end to Angelina and my pops that things would somewhat go back to normal.

I'd just made it back to my office after making sure the staff were on point when my phone trilled with a call from Ava, and I shook my head. I couldn't even be mad because she'd given me way more time than we'd discussed, but I still felt a sense of dread behind going home. A part of me wanted to let it go to voicemail so I didn't have to hear her chew me out until I walked through the door, but I answered anyway and immediately sat up in my chair at the sound of wails in the background.

"Hello, Ava?"

"Yeah, uh, Knight, you need to get home *now*...The hospital just pronounced Ka'Leigh dead."

CHAPTER SIXTEEN
BLESSING

I sat in the first row of the church's pews behind sunglasses but I still couldn't bring myself to open my eyes. I didn't want to see my baby in a fucking casket. I didn't want to see the pictures of him that Knight and Ava had put up and I didn't want to be touched. As sad as I was behind having to bury my baby, I was even more angry. I was angry about so much that I couldn't even pinpoint an exact thing that would drive me over the edge. I kept wondering when I'd explode on any of the people around me. In my mind, I wondered why any of us deserved to be here when Kal wasn't, and then I'd feel bad for thinking something so horrible. I honestly would've preferred that God had just taken me instead so that my baby had a chance, but He'd made his choice and for some fucked-up reason, it was my baby being put to rest.

Ava squeezed my hand, bringing me back to the moment, and I resisted the urge to break her damn fingers. She'd been nothing but supportive and helpful this whole time, even more so than Knight, but that didn't stop me from hating the fact that she was breathing and my baby wasn't. I knew I'd lost my damn mind the minute I considered buying a spell book and sacrificing one of the people in attendance just to have my son back, because shit like that only happened in horror movies, but that's what it felt like I was in. Only in a fucked-up movie could my baby be laying in a casket in front of me, or maybe it was a nightmare that I couldn't wake up from. I squeezed my eyes shut tighter and dug my nails into my hand so deep that I was sure to draw blood, but when I opened my lids I was still in the same church, facing my baby's casket.

My line of sight got blocked and I blinked as Knight stopped in front of me holding Ky. He knew better than to hand him to me so instead, he set him in Ava's arms even though he tried to reach out for me. I couldn't touch him. Hell, I could barely look at him, but it wasn't because I was mad at him, it was because it didn't feel right to have one without the other, and that thought had me feeling guilty as hell. I wondered if he would have survivor's remorse for being the twin that made it. Would he hold some type of resentment toward me for letting his brother die?

"Bless, they're about to end the service. Do you want to go up before they take him away?" Knight's voice broke through my thoughts and I stared at him blankly behind my shades. They were about to take my baby away and he was standing there freshly shaved and smelling like heaven, as if our son wasn't about to be laid to rest. I wanted to slap him—no, I wanted to *kill* him because as much as I felt like this was my fault, I felt like it was his even more. *He'd* allowed that bitch to get away with so much that she felt untouchable. *He'd* allowed her to stay knowing that she was a demon, and *he'd* allowed her to get away. She was probably somewhere laughing at my pain and the fact that he hadn't even tried to catch up to her.

Tears slipped down my cheeks as I shook my head, refusing

to get up. I couldn't let the last memories of my baby be of him like that. I wouldn't. No one was going to make me go up there. I was thankful when Knight finally released a deep sigh and got the fuck out of my face. He'd been steering clear of me and I was thankful for that, because if he spoke too many words to me I'd probably end up in jail for murder. I sat back gripping the pew as if somebody was going to rip me away from it and closed my eyes back as Knight, Bishop, and Rook went up to the casket. I was hoping that when I opened them again they'd have removed it already, even if I had to sit there like that for the next hour.

Ky began crying and I felt Ava get up to take him away, but I still kept my eyes shut. Even when Deja and Golden both came and whispered their condolences to me, I didn't look. Music began playing, "One Sweet Day" to be exact, and a scream erupted from my throat that I felt in the pits of my stomach. I knew I hadn't been any help with the preparations, but *that* song was not what I needed to hear at the moment. It was literally the straw that broke the camel's back, and I screamed trying to drown it out as Deja and Golden attempted to lift me from my seat. I easily broke away and opened my eyes in time to see Rook and Bishop carrying the small baby blue casket.

"No! Nooooo, don't take my baby!" I shrieked, running over to them. I threw myself on top of the casket, clutching it tightly as I cried. "Does he even have a blanket? It's about to be cold, he's going to need a blanket and a hat! Y'all muthafuckas want to put him in the ground so bad you're not even trying to make sure he'll be comfortable!" I sent an accusing glare their way, not caring about the silent tears they were crying. It was fuck them tears and fuck them! They'd stopped to let me cry over my son's body but they wouldn't allow me to take it away from them. We struggled for I don't know how long before Knight finally came over and pulled me away. He tried to whisper soothingly in my ear but I wasn't trying to hear shit! All I wanted was my baby back and since he couldn't do that or even bring the person responsible to meet the same fate, I had nothing for him. "Get the fuck off me! This is all your fuckin' fault! You got us into this mess and now my baby's paying for it!" I fought as hard as I could but he only held me tighter as they finally walked past me carrying Kal.

"I know baby, I know. I'm so sorry." His voice cracked in my ear and I broke down completely, causing us both to land in a heap on the floor as I reached out to his brothers' retreating backs for my baby.

I don't know how much time had passed, but judging by the darkened room I was in it had to be hours. I could barely lift my head from the pillow and my sore eyes took forever adjusting to the dark, but after a while I realized I was in our bedroom. Looking at the clock on the side table, I was able to make out that it was a little after two in the morning and I laid back down. I was thankful that whoever had put me to bed had taken the liberty of undressing me, because I wouldn't have to get up to put on something comfortable. I didn't plan on getting up until Knight brought me Angelina. With my baby more than likely buried, the only thing I could feel right then was a burning rage that wasn't going to go away until I felt that bitch's life slipping away through my fingers, and I'd probably still be angry after that. Really, I wanted her whole bloodline to die just because they were related to her, but because that wasn't necessarily an easy task, I would settle for her alone. I had given Knight time to find her already and for some reason he was coming up short every time, but I knew I wouldn't be able to rest until he granted my request. Closing my eyes, I fantasized about how I would do it. Angelina didn't deserve a quick death like she'd robbed my son of. She deserved to be waterboarded, sliced up, and have lemon juice squirted on her wounds. I couldn't decide which was more horrible so I surmised that they all would do and hopefully, she wouldn't die from the shock before I was ready. The thought was enough to get me back to sleep.

CHAPTER SEVENTEEN
KNIGHT

I stormed into our bedroom holding a crying Ky and looked at Blessing in anger. She'd been in the same spot in the same clothes for the past two weeks and although I truly felt for her, it was time she got her ass up before I committed her. I felt like a disgruntled baby mama as I watched her drool on her pillow like she hadn't just hear Ky screaming at the top of his lungs. She'd been refusing to hold or interact with him since before the funeral, and I knew that a lot of what was wrong with him was because of her shunning him. No doubt he was confused after losing his twin and his mother's sudden absence, but that shit was going to end immediately.

"Blessing! Blessing!" I shouted, and she groaned, turning away from me like that was going to make me go away. I admit it had been working for the last couple of weeks, but I wasn't leaving until she beat this shit. Ava had tried to stay for as long as she could but she eventually had to go home, and in her absence I was playing daddy daycare, maid, housekeeper, cook, and everything else. While I enjoyed spending time with my son, I still needed to be out in the field looking for both Angelina and my pops in addition to running the business. Rook and Bishop had both stepped up in a major way when it came to running things, but they could only do so for so long without me doing my part, and that's where Blessing came in. It was about more than just her looking after Ky though. She'd let herself go. She wasn't eating like she should and she wasn't even showering, and I was at my wits end. I'd already come to the conclusion that she was going to have to talk to somebody, either a grief counselor or a regular old therapist, but she needed help and as the man in her life, I was going to make sure it happened.

"Blessing, get up!" I barked, and she finally tossed the covers off and glared at me from the bed.

"Whaaaaat! Can't you see I'm trying to sleep!" The seriousness of her statement had me chuckling bitterly as I tried to calm myself down. I wasn't trying to argue with her, I was trying to get her to take care of herself and get better for Ky, but it was looking like I would have to have some niggas dressed in white come and cart her ass out of there.

"It's damn near 4 p.m. Bless, you've been in bed all day and Ky's been looking for you. I know you heard his little ass crying." Her nose turned up at that and she rolled her eyes.

"You heard him too which is why you got him. You're his father, right? The one that came all the way to Georgia to get us? You tellin' me you can't handle a crying baby now?" she huffed, unbothered by the fact that Ky was still crying and reaching out for her as we spoke. In fact, she kept her eyes off him completely as if she was afraid to look at him. She'd been doing that shit for weeks and honestly, I was tired of it.

"You're right, I am his father, but you're his mother whether you want to be at the moment or not! You've been neglecting him for weeks and he misses you, so since you won't go to him, I'm bringing him to you," I said, placing Ky down on the bed and damn near bolting out the door while she screamed for me to come back. I made it out of the house in record time and was already pulling out of the driveway when she finally reached the door. Whatever she was saying was lost behind the glass of my car as I sped away, saying a silent prayer that I was pushing her in the right direction.

I was supposed to be meeting my brothers at the club since we'd gotten a hit on King, and I was more than a little thirsty to catch up with him. As I drove, I ignored calls from Blessing, making it to my destination in half the time I normally did. As soon as I walked in, I headed straight up to Bishop's office where I knew they were and let myself in.

"It's about time you got here, nigga," Rook huffed as soon as I walked through the door, and I shot him the finger, taking up one of the free seats in the room.

"Fuck you, I wasn't trying to bring Ky in here so I had to wake up Blessing so I could go." That immediately had both of them looking at me with raised brows.

"You left him with Bless? You sure he's gone be straight?" Bishop was the first to say what was on both of their minds, and I couldn't help the frown on my face. No lie, after the funeral we were all concerned about Blessing's mental state considering how she'd blacked out, but I wasn't worried in the least that she would bring any harm to Ky. I figured the reason she was so comfortable ignoring him was because she always had someone around willing to pick up her slack, so with her being alone she wouldn't have a choice but to take care of him.

"She ain't gone hurt him, nigga. I wouldn't have left him if I thought she would, but I do have cameras up so I'll just check in on him every so often." I pulled up my app to show him the view of Blessing who was now sitting on the couch with a still crying Ky, but at least she was holding him. Bishop still looked at me like I was crazy while Rook did the same, shaking his head.

"I don't know bro, let me just have the Golden go check on her real quick just in case she needs something—"

"No. Blessing's stronger than this shit, just give her some time to rise to the occasion before y'all count her out," I said with finality. I knew my girl better than anybody. She was my best friend before she was my woman and I knew just how strong she was. She could and she would beat this depression and I was going to make sure she did. With that understood, I changed the subject, because we needed to move on King ASAP before he could sneak off to somewhere else. I'd been just as devoted to finding him as I had Angelina and we'd finally pinned him down. He'd been in Hawaii the whole time like he was on vacation while I was burying my son and keeping the secret of Bishop's paternity to myself. Not to mention the charges he was running from, but unfortunately, he would never see a day behind bars.

"I already booked a flight out for tomorrow for all three of us," Bishop spoke up, and I narrowed my eyes at him.

"We can't all go, somebody gotta stay here just in case anything jumps off."

"Hell naw, you think I'm gone miss this shit after everything that nigga did? You definitely smoking dope, bro." Rook shook his head. "And Bishop ain't even never liked his ass so you know he ain't gone be cool with sitting out."

Sighing, I sat back in my chair. I understood exactly where he was coming from because Knight had tried to fuck all of us, so we all deserved to be there to see his last breath. "Ayite, but we need to make it quick, especially since we won't be able to get his ass back here," I conceded, and Rook's crazy ass cheesed like he'd won a prize.

"That's what the fuck I'm talkin' 'bout!" He nodded happily as Bishop began going through the game plan.

THE NEXT NIGHT...

We sat in a safe house a few miles away from where King was holed up going over the final plans, and I could hardly contain myself. I'd been waiting to put a bullet between my father's eyes for the last few weeks and being so close had me anxious and my trigger finger twitched involuntarily.

"Okay, so one last time—"

"Nah, fuck that! We got this shit down muthafucka, let's go!" Rook cut Bishop off, gaining an annoyed look from him.

"We already just barely got away with the shit in Miami 'cause of your poor ass planning, nigga. The least you could do is make sure everything goes off without a hitch. I ain't tryna get locked up or killed out here before I get to see my baby," Bishop scolded, and I sighed and stood up from the couch.

"It's cool, we already know what to do." I tucked my gun and flipped up my hoodie, deading the conversation. They could go back and forth for hours if I let them and I was trying to get this over with tonight so we could move on to the next target. Rook stood next, following me to the door with Bishop right behind him. We all piled into the Jeep we had for the occasion with me behind the wheel and drove the short distance to the resort King was staying in. He'd picked a perfect vacationing spot, probably hoping to blend in with the crowd, but he'd fucked up by having some money wired to himself from one of the bank accounts he didn't know I was aware of. Money was the reason he was even in this whole mess and money was about to be the reason he died.

Parking up the street, we all walked the rest of the way and hit the side door where we were met by one of the maids. She'd been all too happy to make a small fortune by turning over a guest and she granted us access before disappearing out of sight. She told us that King had been spending a lot of his time and money messing with the young island girls and that's where he was currently, in one of the lower rooms that he'd paid up for a month with one of the women he called on. We made our way down the back stairs, making sure to steer clear of any cameras as we slipped on our masks and approached the door.

Music was blasting from the other side, so even when Bishop kicked the door in no one was alarmed. Since he was in a suite, we had to travel through the makeshift living room to get to the bedroom, and I turned my nose up under my mask at how messy that shit was. He had everything from clothes to fast food all over and I had to shake my head at how low he'd sunken. The King I knew would've never lived in such conditions, but he wasn't the King I knew. He was a snake that didn't deserve to be among the living a moment longer. Creeping up to the door, I signaled for my brothers to step aside as I shot off the doorknob, gaining us entry. The silencer on my gun stopped anyone from knowing what was going on aside from the two people in front of us. The girl screamed and immediately tried to cover herself while King reached on the side of the chair he was sitting in, but I quickly sent a bullet through his shoulder, stopping him.

"Get out, go!" Bishop ordered the girl, and she hurried out, leaving her clothes and anything else she might've brought with her.

"Well, well, well, if it ain't the biggest snake himself." I stopped in front of him and removed my mask with a smirk while King grimaced. "You thought you found you the perfect hiding spot, huh?"

"Stop toying with that nigga and shoot his ass!" Bishop

growled, but I ignored him, focusing only on the nigga before me.

"You got anything to say for yourself after all the shit yo' ass been doin'? Tryna set up your sons, taking part in the killing of your grandson." I tsked, shaking my head. "That's some bad karma for yo' ass." I raised my gun, preparing to put every last bullet into his head.

"Fuck you and that little bastard! You ruined my legacy over some twins that you didn't even know were yours and an old piece of pussy! All of y'all did!"

"Cut the shit, King, I know you were tryna set us up to take the fall with Angelo. Wasn't gonna be no legacy if shit went yo' way," I said as he shifted his eyes before once again reaching to the side, and I shot his ass in his other shoulder, making him cry out. "You was gone send yo' own kids up the river for some shit you did. That's fucked up. You know Mama would've never been down with none of that shit."

"None of y'all wanted to make money! Look around nigga, sex trafficking is the new get rich quick scheme. Fuck gambling and strippers when niggas is dying to pay for pussy! Y'all dumb as y'all mama thinking it wasn't worth the risk when I brought in millions off that shit after just a year. I was gonna bring you boys in but yo' mama refused the idea, and I knew if she wasn't with it then y'all wasn't gonna be with it!" he hissed before snapping his mouth shut like he'd said too much.

My eyes narrowed as I pieced together what he was saying at the same time as Bishop, who immediately passed me up and started beating him with the butt of his gun. "What you say! What!" he growled as he tried to choke King's ass, but I pulled him away.

"She was dying anyway!" King panted, spitting out blood, and before he could say anything else Bishop was unloading his clip in him. His body shook as each bullet hit him until there were no more and he fell from his chair. Still even after he was long gone, Bishop continued pulling the trigger as tears streamed down his face. We were all silent, letting it sink in that our father had killed our mama over something so stupid and was now dead too.

I don't know how long passed before I finally took the gun from his hand and pulled him away. For certain, I wasn't going to add to his pain by ever revealing the truth of his paternity now. I could only hope that being the one to end King would bring him the solace he deserved.

CHAPTER EIGHTEEN
BLESSING

I sat sipping wine as Golden did my hair and Deja polished my toes. They called themselves trying to make me feel better, but being pampered didn't do anything but make me feel guilty. I didn't think I should've been able to enjoy anything while Kal was dead, but they'd insisted since the guys had left to find their father. After abandoning me with a crying baby, Knight had sent the girls over to keep me company and probably to make sure I didn't harm myself or Ky. At first I was pissed. I didn't want to be responsible for him, not by myself, but being alone with him forced me to jump right back into mama mode. There wasn't anybody else there to pick up my slack so I couldn't ignore him, and although I was still sad, I picked him up. I fed him and I even played with him until he fell asleep. It didn't take much to fall right back into my role as his caregiver, surprisingly, and as much as I hated Knight at the moment, I had to admit that he'd made the right call by forcing my hand.

"There you go, all done. Now don't get to moving around a whole lot while they dry," Deja ordered, standing up and

FIRST COME THUGS, THEN COME MARRIAGE 4   109

stretching. Her baby bump was becoming a little more evident, or it might've just been me knowing that she was pregnant, but I could clearly see her belly forming. A pang of sadness shot through me remembering when I was pregnant and how the boys kept my ass running to the bathroom.

"She'll be fine, I use that polish all the time and mine dries pretty quick," Golden chimed in, and I sighed, tuning out their conversation. Even though we had been with the guys about the same amount of time, I felt like I should warn them. It was great to be in love, but not if you were losing things because of it, and messing around with the Grand men, they were sure to lose a lot, especially Deja who would be bringing in a child. With the way Bishop's temper was set up, there was no telling how many enemies he'd made, and not to mention the fact that just like Knight, he'd married into a mafia family so there was that risk as well. I wasn't even sure that she and Bishop were together, but even if they weren't, minus the twins, our situations were very similar and I'd rather save her the heartache. Taking another sip of my wine, I prepared to tell her what I was thinking when Ky began crying, and I jumped up to go get him. He'd already fallen back into the routine of me being the one to come running when he cried, and as soon as I entered he was cheesing, even as he blinked his wet eyelashes at me.

"Hey man, what's wrong?" I cooed, lifting him out of the crib and lightly bouncing him, immediately noting the stench coming from his diaper. "Ohhhh, you're a stinky man, that's what's wrong. Well, Mommy will fix that right now." While I talked I gathered a diaper and some wipes before laying him down on his changing table.

In no time he was clean and fresh, and I snuggled him to me, inhaling his baby scent. I got lost in the moment, preferring to spend my time with him instead of the two hopelessly in love women down the stairs. They'd been trying their best but I almost would've preferred for Knight's ass to be there. At least he'd leave me alone once he saw I didn't want to be bothered. Deja and Golden just kept right on going as if they didn't give a damn that I was being antisocial. Here I was trying to have a pity party and they were trying to turn it into a sleepover.

"Blessing, the food's here!" I heard Deja calling, and immediately my stomach growled. It had been hard to eat and I'd been pecking away at anything that was set before me, but the hunger pain that coursed through me at the moment let me know that my body wasn't going to take too much more of my shit. With Ky on my hip babbling, I ambled back downstairs, instantly smelling the Chinese food they'd ordered, and my stomach roared this time. They were already spreading everything out on the table when I appeared, and they both looked up at me with smiles.

"I'll make your plate so you don't have to struggle with Ky," Golden said, already reaching for the plate, but I stopped her.

"I got it."

I could feel their eyes on me as I sat Ky down in his highchair and began putting some of the beef fried rice on my plate along with wings before drenching it in sweet and sour sauce. They tried to make small talk, which wasn't very casual, about Golden's escape and how she'd refused to leave Miami until she found her stepdaughter's mother. Despite my current state, I was glad that she'd gotten away from Diego and that we were no longer hiding out in fear of him, I just wished Kal had also made it out.

Blinking back tears, I kept my eyes on my plate as I forced a spoonful of rice into my mouth. It seemed like just the thought of him had me emotional and I wondered when that would no longer be the case. The way I was feeling right then, I'd be crying forever and I didn't know if that was normal. Every-body, even Knight, seemed to have gone back to life as usual, but I felt stuck in limbo. I didn't want to run my business, I didn't even want to do regular shit that was a part of life. If I could, I'd die right along with my baby.

"Ahahaha, Mama!"

As if Ky could hear my inner thoughts, he started yelling and slamming his little fists on his tray, making my head snap in his direction. Instinctively, I put some of my food in front of him, but he swiped it to the floor, still going off until I finally took him out and sat back down with him in my lap. He imme-diately calmed down and snuggled against me, holding on for dear life. I held him just as tightly, realizing that I'd just been considering killing myself as if he wasn't still here needing me just as much if not more than Ka'Leigh. What type of mother was I that I completely disregarded my living son because of my grief over losing his brother?

"I'll get it." Deja jumped up from the table and left the room. I guess someone was at the door, but if it wasn't Ava I didn't really care. Instead of concerning myself with who it was, I went back to eating and holding Ky until the unmistak-able voice of my mother floated into the room. I hadn't seen or spoken to my parents since that disaster of a lunch and I hadn't made any plans to.

"Oh, Blessing honey!" My mama came right in, throwing her arms around me, and I fought the urge to shrug her off. She hadn't really done anything besides not speak up for me when my father was talking crazy, but I still felt a way about it, which was why I hadn't allowed Ava to invite them to the funeral or even let them know of Kal's passing. I didn't feel like they deserved any information about my personal life after the things that were said. "If I had known I would've been here in a heartbeat! You shouldn't have had to go through this alone," she cried, still wrapped around me. It was on the tip of my tongue to tell her that if she hadn't allowed her husband to cause a wedge between us then I wouldn't have had to go through shit alone. I was wondering how she'd even found out in the first place, and I bit the inside of my cheek, wishing she'd release me and just sit her ass down.

"Where's that *boy*? I know he didn't leave you alone already during such a time." I was both shocked and annoyed to hear my father's voice, and I craned my neck to see him tensely standing just in the entryway.

"Don't start honey, we just got here and Blessing doesn't need that negativity." My mama finally let me go and stood upright to address him. Instead of arguing like I thought he would, his jaw tightened and he looked away, focusing on the crown molding. "How are you girl's doing? I appreciate you being here during my baby's time of need." She turned to the girls with a forced smile.

"It's no problem, we all loved Kal and we love Blessing, so it's only right," Deja spoke up, looking at me from where she sat across the table while Golden nodded in agreement. It was like she was talking directly to me to let me know that's how she felt.

"Well, is there anything you need me to do? Laundry, dishes, I can even take Ky for a little bit if you'd like?" I hadn't really paid much attention to anything besides my food when I'd come down, but it was obvious that Golden and Deja had already cleaned up the kitchen. Knight didn't know it, but I sometimes came down to get water and I saw the mess that had grown since Ava's departure. She'd been a godsend picking up my slack and now the girls had also chipped in. Even if they hadn't though, I doubted I'd let my mama do it and I damn sure wasn't giving her my baby.

"Actually, everything's already done but you're more than

welcome to have dinner with us," Golden said, and I shot her friendly ass a look. I didn't know how long it would be before either of my parents said something that would piss me off and I didn't want to give them a chance to. Despite some intrusive thoughts, I'd been better than I had been yesterday and even the day before that. The last thing I wanted was for my father to say something slick and I curse him the fuck out like he wasn't shit to me. Before I could object, my mama was pulling out the chair next to me and beckoning for my daddy to take a seat as well. He took his time going around to sit across from us, and I rolled my eyes at how uncomfortable he looked. Besides the smart shit he'd said when he first came in, he still had yet to speak and was actively avoiding looking at me. An awkward silence filled the room as we all went back to eating and I was fine with that. I barely wanted them there and I damn sure didn't want to pretend that everything was okay between us, but leave it to my mama to "break the ice."

"So how do you guys know each other?" she asked as she made herself a plate.

"Um, I'm married to Knight's brother Rook, and Deja here is with his other brother, Bishop," Golden proudly said, making my father grunt.

"Oh, that's nice. It's good to be able to get along with your in-laws." My mama tried to talk over him but of course, he wasn't having that.

"Blessing isn't her in-law."

"Phillip, *please*," my mama begged, trying to hide her discomfort behind a smile.

"What? It's the truth. Knight is married but it's not to Blessing so she's not her in-law, the other girl is." He had the nerve to look as if he hadn't just said anything wrong and while I wasn't on good terms with Knight, he had no business bringing that shit up.

"Are you fuckin' serious? I just lost my baby, your grand-son, and you're worried about me and his father's marital status? You haven't even given your condolences but you're in our house talking crazy! The very least you can do is act like you give a fuck about what I'm going through! If you can't do that then you can get the hell out!" My outburst had Ky jumping and he began to cry as my father's face twisted angrily.

"You cursing your parents now? I'm just stating facts, and the fact is you're not the girl's in-law! Now you can play house and pretend all you want, but that's what it is and Ka'Leigh's death is a direct result of y'all living in sin! It's a blessing karma didn't take Ky as well, but nothing is going to go well for you until you get out of this situation!"

"Oh hell naw, that's enough! Sir, you need to leave right now!" Deja stood, looking like she was ready to go to war with him. I was too appalled to even think of anything to say. I didn't expect my father to be harboring such thoughts, but to say that shit aloud and to me was crazy as hell.

"Honey, this is a family matter and—" my mama tried to intervene, but Deja quickly cut her off.

"Lady, Blessing *is* my family and if you and your crazy ass husband don't get the hell out of here, it's gonna be a prob-lem!" Her threatening tone had my mother terrified as she quickly stood on shaky legs.

"Mmph! You see the type of people you're surrounding yourself with? You don't care that she just threatened your parents?"

"Oh, it's not a threat," Deja told my father calmly, before reaching down into her bag and producing a gun that had both my parents gasping. The way he shuffled around the table and gathered his wife was comical, and I burst out laughing as they scrambled from the room. The door slamming loudly behind them had me laughing even harder and before I knew it, Deja and Golden had joined in. "I'm sorry boo, I wasn't really gonna shoot them but your daddy had that coming," she finally said, dropping back into her chair.

"And did!" Golden added with a shake of her head. I couldn't lie, I'd hoped that at some point my father would've apologized for his previous behavior and that my mother would've grown a backbone. It was crazy that he disliked Knight so much that he doubled down even during my time of grief. At least I had some family in my corner that cared about me and would ride this thing out. That was all I needed.

CHAPTER NINETEEN
DEJA

I t didn't take a rocket scientist to figure out that Bishop was the reason my deed ended up in my mailbox or that my mama and sister just up and disappeared. The police had come to inform me that Drea appeared to have burned her house down before going on the run with her husband and our mama, but I knew the truth. What's crazy is that after what they'd done and were planning to do, I didn't even care. That still didn't mean that I was willing to take his lying ass back, especially since he was still married to the bitch that caused my accident. We didn't run in the same circles but if I ever caught up to her, I was going to shoot the fuck out of her, to hell with the consequences.

I'd been holed up with Golden trying to keep an eye on Blessing while Knight was out of town, and I was glad his ass had finally returned. My girl wasn't as bad as the first day we came but she still wasn't her old self and I didn't think she ever would be, but that was to be expected. I didn't know anything about losing a child and so tragically, so I couldn't begin to put myself in her shoes, but from what I could see she was handling it well. She was eating again, taking care of Ky, and doing things around the house, but the way she kept that boy on her hip I knew she was clinging to him out of fear. Before I left I let him know that he should probably get her somebody to talk to because while I didn't expect her to be open about her feelings to us, she did need to get things off her chest in a healthy way. Thankfully, he wasn't one of those niggas that thought therapy was only for white people and he agreed with me, promising to look into it. That was all I could hope for because I still needed to get my life back on track as well.

Even though I had my house, I was still out of a studio. As bad as I missed photography though, I wasn't about to hold shoots at my house or anywhere for that matter after the attempt on my life. Instead, I did landscape pieces and still shots that I sold to commercial companies to bring in some type of money until I felt comfortable meeting with people again. I was at the bank depositing my latest check and then I was going to my first doctor's appointment finally. Even though I'd been on the fence about keeping my baby, I couldn't pretend like I wasn't excited and nervous at the same time. This baby was all I had at the moment and I wanted to make sure I took good care of it, which I hadn't really been doing between fighting my mama and sister and stressing over my life. The last thing I wanted was to end up like Angelina and find out that something was wrong. I honestly wouldn't have been able to handle something like that.

"Here's your receipt with your new balance. Have a good day, Ms. Brooks," the teller said, handing me the receipt before motioning to the next person to step up. Absentmindedly, I glanced at the total and blinked rapidly before turning right the fuck back around. There had to be some type of mistake, because there wasn't any way that many zeros were in my account unless they'd allowed some fraud shit to take place.

"Sorry, this will only take a second," I told the man who'd already stopped at the window, gaining an annoyed look, but I still stepped in front of him unfazed. "This is a mistake, either it's some fraud shit goin' on or y'all got my account mixed up with somebody else's." I took the opportunity to look at the account numbers and confirmed that they were mine, meaning it wasn't a mix up. Somebody was playing with my account.

"Um, ma'am, there's no mistake. This is your account, but I can look into your recent deposits if you'd like?" the teller said, wide eyed.

"Could you please?" I delivered a phony smile and rolled my eyes once she walked off, even though I knew this wasn't her fault. I tried to think of if my mama and sister had somehow done anything fraudulent to my bank account, because I wasn't trying to go to jail along with their asses. Having a baby behind bars wasn't my idea of good parenting, especially when it was over something I didn't have shit to do with.

The girl returned a moment later with an older man who was probably the bank manager, and I braced myself. "Ms. Brooks, I'm Robert, the branch manager. Alicia here told me you have some concerns about your account? If you come with me to my office we can try to sort this out."

I immediately let out a puff of air and rolled my eyes, but I still followed him to his office. This was supposed to be a quick trip before my doctor's appointment and it was turning into a whole thing. I took a seat across from him just as my phone rang, and I quickly ignored it once I saw Bishop's name. He'd been calling me since they returned and I'd been actively paying him dust. Just because he'd gotten my house back didn't mean I was fucking with him like that and I didn't plan to anytime soon.

"Okay, what's the account number?"

I recited the ten-digit number and continued ignoring Bishop's calls since he was now on his third one. I tried to focus on what Robert was saying as he looked at his screen and clicked around on the keyboard. I tucked my phone between my thighs until my phone stopped going off, and I breathed a sigh of relief.

"Well, it looks like there's been quite a few deposits in the last month." He cleared his throat, turning the screen toward me. "They're coming from a Grand LLC, so that's probably why they weren't flagged." As soon as he said Grand, I shook my head with a scoff. Of course, Bishop was behind this shit. It definitely made sense because that was right around the time that I'd found out about the baby.

Before he could say anything else, the door swung open and in walked Bishop with Alicia on his trail. "Sir, I told him to wait but—"

"Why you ignoring my calls?" he quizzed, cutting the girl off as he mugged me.

"Are you crazy! How did you even find me?" It seemed like I always asked his psycho ass the same questions and he always looked at me the exact same way, like I should know better.

"I'm crazy as fuck, you should know that by now as well as that I'm always watching." He shrugged casually, and Alicia's eyes bugged out even more. "Now what's taking so long and why you ignoring my calls, when we got a doctor's appointment to go to?" Flabbergasted, my jaw dropped and I looked to Robert for some type of help.

"Sir, I'm going to have to ask you to—"

"Don't ask me shit! You fuckin' with this nigga, Dej? Is that why you in here closed up in his office?"

I couldn't even do shit but laugh. There was no other way to react to such craziness, and even though I didn't want to give these people a show, it was obvious that Bishop was ready to show his ass. Robert began pleading his case immediately as I stood up, blocking Bishop's view of him.

"I'm back here because somebody decided to deposit a hundred thousand dollars into my account without telling me." Folding my arms, I cocked my head, looking up at him, and he finally relaxed, taking his eyes off of Robert.

"I forgot about that," he admitted with a shrug, and while I already knew dealing with Bishop would be different, I couldn't help but wonder what type of money these niggas really had if he could drop six figures in my account and completely forget about it.

"Well, I'm sending it back and you can give it to Lovelie," I lied straight through my teeth. I was a lot of things, but I wasn't a damn fool. We had a baby on the way and whether I wanted to forgive him or not, I was going to accept any money, gifts, or baby items because my kid deserved the best and they were going to get it. He sighed at Lovelie's name, or maybe at me saying I was giving the money back.

"Don't listen to her ass, leave the money where it's at and expect another deposit soon." That was directed at Robert before Bishop grabbed my arm and ushered me out of the office and to the parking lot. I didn't put up a fight because all eyes were already on us, but once we neared my car I snatched away.

"I'm not yo' wife, *Bishop*! You don't get to tell me what to do! I didn't even say anything about this appointment because I wanted it to be peaceful—"

"No, you wanted me to believe that you'd aborted my fuckin' baby! Unfortunately for yo' ass, I got eyes and ears everywhere so I knew you hadn't been to any of the clinics out here. Now let's go, 'cause we're already late." Goofy ass nigga even opened my door and everything. Since I didn't have an argument, I got in with an attitude and allowed him to close the door, watching him cross the parking lot to get back to his car. I considered taking my ass home instead of doing what he said, but that wouldn't do anything but make me miss my appointment and I wasn't going to penalize my baby for their crazy ass daddy.

CHAPTER TWENTY
BISHOP

Deja thought she was slick scheduling her appointment and not saying shit to me, but I hoped now she understood the lengths I'd go through to be a part of our baby's life. Money in her account was nothing to me, neither was having her phone bugged and hacked so her location was on at all times. She pretended to have an attitude about me popping up on her but once we got to the doctor's office, she was unable to hide her excitement. I couldn't lie, I felt the same, and once I heard our baby's heartbeat and saw it on the screen, it was even more amazing than I thought it'd be. The experience had me making sure Deja got home safe and then going to have a word with God, some shit I hadn't done in a while.

I pulled up to the nearest church and I was thankful it wasn't any services going on at the moment, so I was alone. Dropping into a pew somewhere in between the altar and the door, I folded my hands, knowing my OG would fuck me up for not addressing Him on my knees but it would have to do.

"I know I'm probably the last nigga that should be coming in here making a request, but I can't risk my shorty paying for my sins. I've done a lot of necessary but fucked-up things and I won't run down the list or nothin', but you know how I give it up." I lowered my voice just in case someone was lurking around. "I need you to look out for my baby, give them a guardian angel or something that'll keep them out of harm's way or will keep any people with ill intent away from them. I'll do my part but I'm only one man. As selfish as it may sound, considering all the hell I've caused, I need you keep him or her out of whatever you may have comin' for me. That's between us. I'll burn in a pit of eternal fire for my discretions but before or even after that happens, you make sure my child is covered. If it helps, I'll try to limit the casualties but I can't make no promises." Looking up at the cathedral ceiling, I quietly said Amen before climbing to my feet. I'd made my request known and all that was left to do was wait.

Leaving the church, I checked in with Deja to make sure she was cool and didn't need anything, even though I'd just left her. Seeing my baby had me ready to hover over her every second of the day, knowing it was impossible. I needed to get her more security ASAP since she wasn't trying to let me near her, but I was only going to allow that for so long.

I watched the bubbles appear as if she was about to reply to my message before they went away. She was playing hard right now but I could understand why. We'd both said shit we didn't mean during our last argument, but regardless of what was said, her ass was carrying my baby, which meant I was going to be around whether she liked it or not. Better yet, I was going to be with her whether she liked it or not.

Since I still had a little time before heading to the restaurant, I decided to drop in on my mama. It had been a while and

King's confession had her heavy on my mind. While I always had my opinions about that nigga, I'd never have suspected that he would do something so fucked up. I was so mad I wanted to dig that nigga up and rebury him for that shit. After all my mama had done, he'd gone and ended her life much sooner than intended, and while she was already suffering through cancer no less. I planned to find her damn nurse and kill that bitch for playing in my mama's face too.

I was at the cemetery in less than an hour and as always, it was nearly empty. Clutching a bouquet of flowers, I made my way to her headstone and frowned when I didn't see the last ones I'd put there. I looked around like the person was still going to be walking around and when I came up empty, I turned my attention back to my OG.

"Damn Ma, these bum ass people out here stealin' yo' shit!" I complained as I set her new flowers down. It was crazy that you had to watch a gravesite in order to stop niggas from disrespecting them. Shaking my head, I released a deep breath. "I saw the baby today and it was wild, we heard the heartbeat and everything. Shit was life changing, had me going in a church and talking to God." I chuckled. "It's crazy how I love the fuck out that lil' baby already and I can't say that my own pops ever felt like that about any of us. That nigga where he belongs though. I hope that helps you to rest easy. Keep an eye on Kal too, OG. I know he's up there with you watching over us, and let him know his justice coming soon."

I stood up, dusting off my jeans before touching her headstone, and went to drop off Deja's grandma's flowers. Unlike my mother's, the ones I'd brought her last lay on her grave untouched and wilting. I quickly swapped them for the new ones and let her know about me and Deja's visit to the doctor. A nigga was too proud and I was probably going to go around talking about it all day.

Ratatatatatatatat!

I'd been in the middle of talking when gunfire erupted, causing me to drop to the ground, but not before a burning sensation tore through my chest. I immediately pulled out my gun and looked around to find out where the shots were coming from and saw a black Durango speeding away. Pain had my body feeling like it was vibrating as I stood up, but I refused to pass out. I shot right back, hitting their back window. They lost control and trampled over graves until they smashed into a tree across the way. Willing myself to stay alert, I hobbled over, clutching the right side of my chest with my gun still tucked securely in my hand. The disrespect was at an all-time high and I needed to make sure that whoever had violated me was dead. The closer I got to the vehicle the more lightheaded I began to feel, but I didn't stop until I was opening up the passenger side door. I instantly recognized one of Pierre's men knocked out cold with his head on the dash. Even as questions lingered in my mind, I shot him in the temple. The driver was already slumped over the steering wheel with a gaping hole coming out the back of his head.

Gritting my teeth to fight off the pain, I leaned up against their truck panting as I tried to hurriedly call Knight before everything went black.

I woke up in a hospital room and squinted at how bright it was in that bitch. The last thing I remembered was calling Knight, and as if I'd called out his name, his big ass appeared at my bedside with. "Hold on." He stopped me from speaking and I realized it was because I had a damn tube down my throat. I'd gotten shot enough times to know that when they did that shit it was serious. I glared at him as he called for a nurse but knew better than to pull that shit out like I wanted to. He kept silent as we waited for the nurse with a serious look on his face. I already knew he was pissed because I was too! And the worst part was that it was my father-in-law's men. I didn't know what to think. On one hand, Pierre could've done this as retaliation for Lovelie, but that wouldn't make sense considering the type of man he was. However, I didn't put shit past anyone.

"Oh, you're awake!" The nurse came in smiling despite the mug I was giving her. "Well, I'm sure you're ready to get that annoying tube out, so I'll do that first and then we'll check your vitals." She made small talk as she gathered what she'd need to remove the tube, unbothered by Knight's limited engagement.

It didn't take her long to finish and in no time, she'd removed the tube and was offering me a cup of water. I gladly accepted, drinking it slow just like she warned me to as she began taking my vitals, and then she finally left promising to return with the doctor soon. I waited until the door closed fully behind her before finally speaking.

"What we bouta do? 'Cause you already know I'm down for whatever," I stated seriously, noting how raspy my voice was. I was ready to shoot some shit up and ask questions later after what had happened to me.

"*We* ain't bouta do shit! Sit this one out and let me handle it." He sliced the air and then palmed his chest. Grimacing, I tried to sit up and was hit with a sharp pain that had me falling back with a groan. "See, that's what the fuck I'm talkin' 'bout. Yo' ass can't even sit up and you think you bouta get in the field?"

"I'm good!" I could barely get the lie out before he was scoffing.

"You're not good, and yo' ass is gone stay in this hospital until they release you, and then you gone rest until you got the okay to move freely."

My face balled up even more and I sucked my teeth irritably. I hated when he used that head of the family ass voice. He thought I was King or Rook and he could tell me what to do, but I didn't give a fuck what he said. I was going to go see about what the fuck Pierre was on.

CHAPTER TWENTY-ONE
DEJA

Bishop had been calling and texting me since the day before and I'd been ignoring the fuck out of him. It was to the point where I was ready to block his ass because he was turning into a whole stalker. He'd just called like three times back-to-back and it was only ten in the morning. I watched as another call rolled in and nonchalantly chewed my bacon. I wasn't in a rush to deal with him again so soon, and I definitely wasn't going to while I was trying to eat.

The next call that came through was from Knight, and that had my eyebrows bunching. He never called me, and while I could assume it was for his brother since his ass was literally just calling, there was a chance it was for Blessing, and I didn't want to take the chance that she needed me. Then again, she was getting back to her old self so I was sure if she did she'd call on her own. I let his call go to voicemail too and continued eating.

"No Baby, quit begging!" I snapped, getting tired of the phone going off and his ass whining at the same time. Scared, he laid down and covered his head, instantly making me feel bad enough to give him the last piece, which he happily gobbled up. His ass loved bacon.

I carried my plate to the kitchen, talking shit under my breath as I did. Without any studio or upcoming jobs, I didn't have shit to do and I planned to stay in the house and relax all day. That's what I was thinking until somebody started banging on my damn door like the police.

"Now who the fuck?"

Storming to the door, I snatched it open ready to curse somebody the fuck out, but the sight of Golden had me frowning in confusion. "Girl, what the hell—"

"Why haven't you been answering yo' damn phone?" she fussed, pushing her way into the house.

"For who, Bishop? I just saw his ass yesterday. Whatever he want, can't be that damn urge—"

"Girl, he was shot at the cemetery yesterday. Where the fuck have you been?" she cut me off with a raised brow, and my heart stopped.

"What the fuck?" The last thing I'd been expecting to come out her mouth was that Bishop had been hurt. I thought for sure he was just being his usual, crazy, stalking self, not that he was laid up with a bullet hole. As mad as I was at him, I didn't want his black ass to die. Frantically, I ran to put on my slides and a hoodie.

"Don't be tryna rush now, whatever he wanted can't be that urgent," she mocked, folding her arms, and I paused briefly to glare her way.

"You're making jokes right now, like my man ain't in the fuckin' hospital shot?"

"Ahhhhh, now he yo' man, huh? I swear I don't want none of that baby daddy love." She clicked her tongue, shaking her head at me. "He's gonna be fine though. He only got hit twice, once in the chest, once in the stomach."

She was talking casually but my eyes bucked at the number of times and the areas. I wasn't a nurse, but even I knew that was a close ass call and he could've really died. Blinking back tears, I snatched up my keys ready to go see him with her right on my heels, still talking shit.

I broke every traffic law I could getting to the hospital and immediately asked for directions to his room. Thankfully, Golden had decided to drive herself because I couldn't take too much more of her shit-talking ass. We all knew if it was Rook and the nigga had only been shot in the pinky toe, she'd be crying a river and falling out everywhere, while she was trying to play it cool.

When I finally got to his room, I breathed a sigh of relief and then busted out crying seeing him sitting up in bed. I wasn't sure what I was expecting, but I didn't think he'd be up talking shit with his brothers like he wasn't in a hospital bed.

"Oh hell no, not Charlie's Angel up in here crying over this nigga!" Rook cracked as I took slow steps toward Bishop, slightly afraid that I'd hurt him if I came in too strong. He had a look of surprise on his face, probably because of the tears, but nevertheless, he beckoned me closer even after I froze up a couple of feet from the bed.

"I'm good Deja, don't start getting all soft on me." He raised a brow, genuinely concerned.

"I just, I've been ignoring you and you could've died!" My voice came out high-pitched, sending his brothers into a fit of laughter. "Fuck y'all, okay! Y'all had a whole day to come to terms with him being shot, I just found out!" By now I was blubbering and Bishop reached out for me, pulling me closer to his side.

"I'm good Dej, stop crying." Using his thumbs, he wiped away my tears and I could clearly see the smirk playing on his lips. "You might as well gone head forgive me now, yo' ass in here bouta have a panic attack over me."

"Shut up!" I sucked my teeth and shoved him, causing his face to contort. "Oh my gosh, I'm so sorry!" I shrieked, slapping my hands over my mouth.

He shifted away from me with a look that could kill, but through gritted teeth he said, "It's cool."

"That boy really love yo' ass, 'cause he in real life pain and you just pushed the shit out him! I know he wanna slap yo' ass for real." Rook's childish ass cackled and Knight shoved him toward the door.

"We gone be back later bro, you need anything?" he asked, pausing in the doorway with raised brows.

"Naw, I'm good." Bishop quickly declined, keeping his eyes on me. Taking the hint, Knight went ahead and ducked out, leaving us alone.

"You sure you're really okay?" I asked after a few seconds of silence, and he blew out a deep breath.

"Yeah, I'm good, just mad as fuck I gotta wait to get my lick back." He sounded like a big baby.

"What you mean your lick back! You were just shot up, the last thing you need to be thinking about is revenge! You can't help me raise a child and be out here like you're living in the Wild West! We could've lost you," I said lowly, having gotten control of my voice even though my heart was constricted. Out of the brothers, Bishop was certainly the wild card and I don't want his need for revenge to send him to his Heavenly Father. His face tightened as he looked away from me.

"I can't make no promises, Dej. An attempt was made on my life, so I gotta follow through and get at them before they fuck around and hurt y'all trying to get to me. It's best to handle shit like this early, and I promise I'll be as cautious as I can be, but I'm doing this for us so we ain't gotta be looking over our shoulders for the rest of our lives."

I honestly hadn't considered me and the baby being in danger too, but that was a strong possibility, especially with his and Knight's crazy ass wives on the loose. Sighing, I nodded my understanding, even though I was scared as hell for him, hell, for all of us. Seeing my doubt, he grabbed my chin, turning me so I could face him.

"On my life, won't shit happen to me. You gotta trust me ... do you?" he asked with raised brows, and I thought for a second on whether or not I should believe his crazy ass when tomorrow wasn't promised to anyone. Still, I ended up nodding because despite everything, he'd always come back to me and I hoped he always would.

CHAPTER TWENTY-TWO
BISHOP

The hospital wasn't trying to release me for a few weeks but I didn't have that long to waste. There was a chance that Lovelie would flee just like Angelina had and I didn't want to risk it, so I'd greased a couple of nurses' palms so I could have a night out. Since Knight was going to be acting like somebody's daddy, I called Rook's goofy ass, and as soon as he heard the plan he was all in. That was exactly what I needed too, because I didn't have time to wait around.

The nurse, Rita, snuck me out of a side emergency door where Rook was waiting beside his car. We had arranged for me to change into a pair of sweats before leaving, so all I needed now was my guns.

"Boy, yo' ass out here looking like the nigga from *Misery*!" Rook cracked from the car, and I resisted the urge to punch him since it'd probably hurt me more.

"Man, fuck you! Where my guns at!"

"I brought these since it's a special occasion." He tossed a couple 9-millimeter handguns into my lap and I checked to make sure the safety was off of them both, even though I'd told his ass to bring something a lot stronger, but they'd have to do. "Where we headed first?" Rook asked, sounding more excited than he should for a trip to go murder some damn body, but I couldn't lie, I was on cloud nine too.

Lucky had finally hit me up with the information I'd been waiting on, and imagine my surprise when I saw that it was Pierre's men who'd run Deja off the road and killed her security. And while I wondered if he'd been the one to put the order out, I quickly found out it was Lovelie. It had always been her ass. I felt stupid as fuck to be honest. I hadn't expected it to be her. I'd given way more credit than she was due, but that shit ended tonight!

We went to Lovelie's house, and the whole ride over I only got more and more pissed off at how she'd played in my face. We pulled up just in time to see her car pulled right up to the door and the trunk wide open. Rook hurried to put the car in park but I was already climbing out, ignoring the burning sensation that shot through my side as I hurried up the walkway with him a few feet behind.

I got to the door just as she was pulling a big ass suitcase to it, and the second she saw me she froze. "Going somewhere?"

"Bishop? I—" she stuttered, looking me over in terror.

"You what?" I advanced on her, and she backed into the house, letting her suitcase go. "You tried to kill my girl, and then you got that ugly ass nigga to try to kill me too? Is that what you were going to say?"

"No! I—"

"You know, ever since Deja's accident, my brothers were telling me to look into you being the source, but I kept saying you'd never go against your father's word. I couldn't believe it when Lucky connected you to old boy, but now it makes perfect sense." I quickly grabbed her by the throat and squeezed, cutting off her air. She struggled to get away, scratching at my hands, but I didn't let her go until her eyes turned red and bulged and her body went limp. Releasing her, I watched her body drop to the floor and pulled out my gun, wanting to make sure she was dead.

"Nigga, yo' ass crazy!" Rook scoffed, looking at me with his face twisted. I knew he was only pissed off because we hadn't gotten all rowdy yet, but I still needed to pull up on Pierre.

"Shut up and call the cleanup crew so we can head to her pops's crib." That had a smile spreading across his face, and he hurried to do just that while I limped out behind him.

The next day I was back in my hospital bed like hadn't shit happened, when Knight stormed into my room with a scowl. "Nigga, you hardheaded as fuck, you know that right!" he went in immediately, and I just shrugged.

"I don't even know what you talking about," I lied, watching as he shook his head.

"You know exactly what I'm talking about, but I'm gone let you make it. We got some other news."

"Oh yeah, what's up?" I sat up in bed, wincing lightly, and he noticed that shit right away.

"Guess who just called Rook." Smirking like a crazy person, he waited for me to actually try to guess.

"Nigga, I ain't doing that shit, just tell me."

"Jules."

I was dumbfounded. I hadn't expected that to be who he was going to say, but now I was really interested since his goofy ass couldn't stop grinning. "Okay, and? What she say?"

"She told us their location, muthafucka! We're off to Jamaica!" His ass was too hype and I completely understood why as I tried to figure out how the fuck I was going to go with them. That bitch Angelina deserved a bullet from everyone in the family, and I needed to be able to see her demise.

"Well, let's fuckin' go!" I went to toss my covers back and he quickly stopped me.

"Naw, not yo' sneaky ass. You already done left the hospital and wreaked havoc on the city with Rook. I got this one," he said, nodding, and I could already see his wheels turning in his head.

"Yeah, ayite. I'm leaving this muhfucka just like I did last time, and I wish yo' big ass would try and stop me," I huffed, ready to argue him up and down.

"Nope, stay yo' handicapped ass here and let Deja take care of you." His ugly ass strolled out of the room just as Deja appeared carrying some food in a Tupperware bowl. I mugged him, wanting to throw something at him, but I let him slide. If he thought they were leaving without me and my girl, they were stupid.

CHAPTER TWENTY-THREE
BLESSING

I wasn't really in a vacationing mood, but I also wasn't going to deny myself the break. I needed a mental getaway. Hell, we all did, so when Knight told me to pack my bags, I did so quickly. Things weren't as bad between us as they had been, but I still wasn't fucking with him like that. We were cordial and we spoke, and were able to take care of Ky together, but I was still waiting on him to right the wrong of what happened to Kal.

I'd just put my baby down to bed when Knight walked into the room dressed in all black. He tossed something on the bed beside me, and I looked to see that it was clothes that were similar to what he was wearing.

"Get dressed, I got a surprise for you," he said simply before leaving the room of our bungalow. I couldn't help being a little confused about what his ass was up to, but I wasn't going to turn down a surprise, so I quickly got dressed, throwing on the leggings and hoodie in seconds. I met him on the deck and froze seeing Bishop and Rook out there with him, and my forehead creased.

"What's going on?" I looked to each one waiting for an explanation, but the only one who spoke was Knight.

"I said it's a surprise. Come on." He reached out his hand to me and I took it cautiously as my heart beat wildly. I didn't know what he had up his sleeve but from the way he was acting, I knew it had to be good. When I was close enough he pulled out a blindfold. "Put this on."

With narrowed eyes, I allowed him to tie the blindfold on me before he led me away. We eventually ducked into a car and were driving for only a few minutes when I finally began to get nervous. "Uhhh, Knight, where are you taking me? Ky's going to wake up soon." My voice shrilled anxiously, and I could hear Rook's childish ass laugh.

"He's okay, Golden got him," he assured, resting his hand on top of mine to comfort me, but I was anything but comfortable. My fear intensified when we finally stopped and I couldn't hear shit but the sound of animals and shit. A man said something in Jamaican that I couldn't understand as Knight guided me by hand through what I could only assume was some fucking wild jungle.

"Ayite, where are you taking me?" Snatching away, I pulled the blindfold off and looked around frantically, but we were surrounded by darkness aside from the flashlights they carried. "Are you trying to kill me?" I shrieked, and this time they all laughed before Knight came closer, crunching leaves as he did.

"Bless, baby, why the fuck would I try to kill you? You think these niggas would help me?" He chuckled, taking my hand. "Just trust me, okay."

I nodded reluctantly and allowed him to guide me further out until we reached a small cabin of some sort. Rook and Bishop stood aside while Knight opened the door, and it was pitch black inside. Looking in foolishly, my face frowned up until I heard light whimpering coming from the darkness.

"Knight? Knight, is that you? Please!"

A gasp escaped me and I looked at him with wide eyes. I knew that raggedy bitch's voice from anywhere. It was Angelina! Knight nodded, seeing the recognition in my eyes, and ushered me inside, finally cutting on the light in the room. He had her and two other women blindfolded and tied to chairs in the middle of the floor. It looked like they'd been there for days and the smell was almost unbearable, but that didn't stop me from stepping closer and snatching that bitch's blindfold off. She blinked rapidly and looked around, eyes bulging as they landed on each one of us, and I met her with an evil smirk.

"Surprise, bitch!" She went to speak and I punched her dead in the mouth, instantly drawing blood. "You thought you were just going to get away with what you did?" I quizzed, hitting her between each word until I was out of breath and she whimpered quietly.

"Please!"

"Oh, please? I know you don't got the nerve to be begging me!" Her voice enraged me more than her tears and I lifted my foot, kicking her dead in her chest and sending the chair flying backward. The other two women screamed hearing her cry out in pain, but I was focused solely on Angelina. I beat her ass until I was too tired to swing while Rook talked shit from behind me. When I finally backed away she was barely conscious, and Knight appeared next to me brandishing a gun.

"You wanna do the honors?" he asked, and my breath hitched in my throat. I hadn't ever imagined killing anyone, but if I was going to, it would be the bitch breathing heavily on the floor. My hesitation only lasted a moment and I took it from him. Walking over to where she was laid out, I stood over her still panting.

"Rot in hell, hoe!" I grit before pulling the trigger until it could only click. At the same time, Rook and Bishop sent single bullets to the other women's heads, and Knight slowly took the gun from me. I didn't realize I was crying until I fell into his arms and tasted the salty tears. It was finally over and I'd finally gotten Kal some justice.

EPILOGUE
ONE YEAR LATER...

"I now pronounce you man and wife! You may now kiss the bride!"

Everyone clapped and cheered as Bishop and Deja shared their first kiss as a married couple. It had been a crazy ass six months leading up to the wedding, but she'd finally made it and she looked beautiful. They were the last to make their nuptials final after me and Knight, and it had turned out just as amazing as we'd envisioned. As usual, Bishop held their baby girl Serenity as they came down from the altar and I couldn't help but laugh. She was definitely going to be spoiled rotten with the way he carried on over her, but it was the cutest thing.

I smiled and held tightly to Ky with one hand and held our own baby girl with the other as the bridal party walked by. She'd just made two months and didn't do anything but sleep still. I hadn't known I was pregnant during everything that was going on and didn't find out until I was almost five months. The stress of Kal's death along with the other shit had me not showing any symptoms, and I was shocked to even find out. At first it threw me into another depression, but after talking to my therapist about it, I realized that Kylee was a blessing and I embraced my pregnancy from that point on.

"Girl, you lookin' good as fuck in that dress. I'm ready to go make another one of these ASAP." Knight broke off from the bridal party and pulled me close. I giggled, but he had me fucked up if he thought I was popping out another baby anytime soon. We already had two kids in diapers and I wasn't beat for another one yet.

"Um, you better hold and cherish these two you got, 'cause ain't gone be no baby making no time soon." I busted his bubble just as Rook and Golden appeared. Since everything happened, they actually really got married and she finally opened up the dance studio that Rook had bought her. She offered everything from pole dancing classes, which me and Deja always attended when I wasn't at work and she wasn't at her new studio to teach ballet for little girls, and I couldn't wait to get our babies in there.

"Do y'all ever get tired of talking like that?" she playfully asked, stroking Kylee's cheek.

"You bouta be next on the roster while you playin'. Might as well get yo' stomach ready 'cause we definitely bouta get pregnant tonight too, shit!" Rook's funny ass said, making her look at him crazy before dragging him off. He didn't know it yet, but she'd just found out she was pregnant and was planning to tell him on his birthday.

"How you feelin', Mrs. Grand?" Knight pulled me into a hug and I couldn't help the smile that erupted across my face from his touch and my new last name.

"I feel...complete." That had his expression matching my own and he dropped a kiss on my lips. We'd definitely come a long way from him kidnapping me and my kids and everything in between, but I was finally at a place where I was happy and I couldn't ask for more.

The end...

ALSO BY J. DOMINIQUE

The Coldest Savage Stole My Heart 2

Made in the USA
Columbia, SC
16 November 2023

26399447R00090